I0582575

SHELBY FERGUSON AMATEUR SLEUTH - 2

INHERIT THE LAND

JOE EDD MORRIS

Black Rose Writing | Texas

©2023 by Joe Edd Morris
All rights reserved. No part of this book may be reproduced, stored in a retrieval system or transmitted in any form or by any means without the prior written permission of the publishers, except by a reviewer who may quote brief passages in a review to be printed in a newspaper, magazine or journal.

The author grants the final approval for this literary material.

First printing

This is a work of fiction. Names, characters, businesses, places, events, and incidents are either the products of the author's imagination or used in a fictitious manner. Any resemblance to actual persons, living or dead, or actual events is purely coincidental.

ISBN: 978-1-68513-303-0
PUBLISHED BY BLACK ROSE WRITING
www.blackrosewriting.com

Printed in the United States of America
Suggested Retail Price (SRP) $19.95

Inherit the Land is printed in Garamond Premier Pro

*As a planet-friendly publisher, Black Rose Writing does its best to eliminate unnecessary waste to reduce paper usage and energy costs, while never compromising the reading experience. As a result, the final word count vs. page count may not meet common expectations.

To Jo Jo

In memory of Lester F. Sumners

PRAISE FOR THE
SHELBY FERGUSON AMATEUR SLEUTH SERIES

"Joe Edd Morris tells a poignant tale of a young man's search for identity... This beautifully-upbeat and enduring novel is recommended for all ages, especially in areas with large Hispanic populations."
–*The Library Journal*

"A truly memorable literary journey... combining a strong plot with first-rate characters and some elegiac writing about the link between families, the land and its history... Morris' obvious talent shines through from start to finish."
–*Publisher's Weekly*

"Morris writes with a clear lyricism... Morris knows Mexico... descriptions of the landscape and the small towns ring of hard-earned observation. He is aware of language and what it can bring to a story and equally cognizant of what it can subtract from a story."
–*Raleigh News Observer*

"*Land Where My Fathers Died* is an amazing debut. It made me think of *All the King's Men*, *Blood Meridian*, even *As I Lay Dying*. Joe Edd Morris's characters spring from the earth itself. This is a book you won't put down. A story you will remember for many years to come. What a novel. What a writer."
–*Steve Yarbrough*

INHERIT
THE
LAND

TEXAS
Eagle Pass
Piedras Negras
MEXICO
Brownsville
Monterrey
Matamoros
Saltillo
San Luis Potosi
Querétaro
Ciudad de México
Cuernavaca
Taxco

Rome
Parchman
Greenville
Mississippi River
LOUSIANA
ALABAMA
MISSISSIPPI
New Orleans
GULF
OF
MEXICO
Vera Cruz

GENEOLOGY

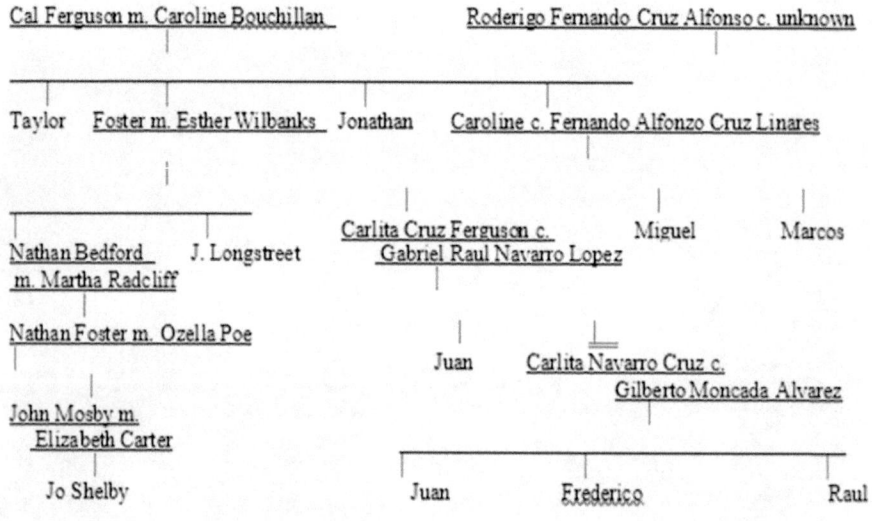

Cal Ferguson m. Caroline Bouchillan   Roderigo Fernando Cruz Alfonso c. unknown

Taylor   Foster m. Esther Wilbanks   Jonathan   Caroline c. Fernando Alfonzo Cruz Linares

Carlita Cruz Ferguson c.   Miguel   Marcos
    Gabriel Raul Navarro Lopez

Nathan Bedford   J. Longstreet
m. Martha Radcliff

Nathan Foster m. Ozella Poe   Juan   Carlita Navarro Cruz c.
                                   Gilberto Moncada Alvarez

John Mosby m.
    Elizabeth Carter

Jo Shelby   Juan   Frederico   Raul

"The righteous shall inherit the land, and dwell therein forever."
–Psalm 37:29

Part I

I

Flat and endless the land swept by, dark and freshly plowed and sweet-smelling, broken now and then by an occasional splash of redbud, the first signs of Delta spring, that world he'd left behind now materializing in his vision. The unchanging horizon, straight as a thread pulled tight. Distant solitary trees. The unpainted ramshackle houses along the highway and the big white-columned ones afar off and the colored people who worked both worlds treading the dusty roads between them. The cotton gins and church steeples, anchors that somehow held it all in place. He began figuring how long it had been, surely years, but six months was all he could total on his fingers.

He asked the man he'd hitched the ride with the date and the man told him Saturday, March twelve, year of our Lord nineteen hundred and fifty-five and asked why he needed to know.

Just wasn't sure if it was yesterday or yesteryear, Jo Shelby said.

The man cast him a puzzled glance and looked back at the highway. He was a large burly man and wore a western-style hat and had a huge mole on the side of his nose. You lost or somethin? the man said.

Nope. Found.

They rode on. Jo Shelby could feel the man sizing him up in the silence. Been away a while, huh?

Yep. You might say that. Seems like more than a while though.

Down south?

Pretty much.

The coast?

Mexico.

Mexico? What the hell you been in Mexico for?

That's where I got found. It's a long story.

The man shook his head, muttered a profanity under his breath and spit out the window of the pickup as it sped down the highway.

They passed Ruleville, then the Drew city limits sign and Jo Shelby asked the man to slow down, that he'd get out there.

Thought you said you were going to Rome, the man said.

I am, he said. Got some business to tend to here first.

Where in town you going? the man said. Don't mind swinging you by. Drew aint but a bump in the road.

Not exactly sure. Thanks all the same.

The man's face screwed up. You getting out here and don't know where you're going? Thought you said you were found.

Oh, I know where I'm going all right. Just don't have it in my sights yet.

The man shook his head as if shaking off a pest. If you don't mind my asking, where do you live in Rome?

He minded but the man had driven him from Indianola and the least he could do was answer his question.

Lived at Jack Patrick's.

Jack Hurley Patrick. I'll say. Good friend of mine. You live on his place?

Did.

You look kinda familiar. What's your name, anyway?

Ferguson. Jo Shelby Ferguson.

Ferguson, the man said, then repeated the name. There was a Ferguson worked there once, managed the place. He and his wife got killed in a car wreck a while back.

Jo Shelby was standing on the graveled shoulder of the road still holding the door open. Much obliged, mister. Think I'll just walk. Like you said, it's a bump in the road, all downhill from here. He closed the door and crossed the road in front of the truck.

Sorry about those other Fergusons, if they were kin to you, the man leaned his head out the window and hollered after him.

Jo Shelby waved a hand of acknowledgment but never looked back, his eyes steady down the macadam road that would take him into town.

Downtown Drew was one long street. On one side was an assortment of mercantile stores, offices, a drug store and the City Café. On the other were the railroad tracks, the same that passed by the penitentiary at Parchman and Rome, extending all the way to Memphis in the north and Jackson in the south and points further, he guessed. To get to Main Street and the tracks he had to pass an odd collection of establishments—a wholesale grocery, cotton mill, silo, service station, body shop, salvage yard, picture show. And the Chinaman's grocery where he went to buy a Coke and candy bar the Saturday night before the Monday he was arrested and had six years of his life stolen from him before the real killer confessed and he was released. By the short arm of the law, cause if it'd been long they'd have gotten it right the first time.

At the Chinaman's grocery he stopped, considered his reflection in the store window. With the sombrero-looking hat he'd bought in Mexico shading his face, its wide brim giving him a touch of gallantry, folks probably wouldn't recognize him. Which was good, for right now anyway.

He crested the tracks, swung his vision left to right along the row of store fronts facing him but saw nothing on any sign that said LAWYER. He crossed the tracks and headed south down Main. At the corner drug store he turned and noted the brick two-story Hickman building across the street, rich written all over it. Planter's lawyer. He walked on.

He'd made half the block on Church Street when he saw a small white sign that said WILLIAM W. DINKLER, Dentist. He marked it in his memory. His front teeth were gone, punched out by a boot toe in the last fight for his life in Mexico. The few times he'd allowed himself a glimpse in a mirror, the gummy gap looked like something cut by a small child in a Halloween pumpkin. They sure to God needed fixing if any serious romancing was to have half a chance.

Several doors down he saw what he was looking for. ATTORNEY AT LAW arched in large gold letters across the plate-glass window, the man's name beneath in smaller letters. Lester E. Darden. He peered through the window and saw a young lady behind a desk typing, a couple of upholstered chairs, an old leather couch, a few pictures on the walls. Nothing fine. He opened the door and went in.

Les Darden, the man said approaching Jo Shelby with a fleshy outstretched hand and broad full-toothed smile. He was portly with silver hair and wore a seersucker suit and red tie and walked with a slight tilt to one side.

He rose from the couch where he'd been waiting. Jo Shelby Ferguson. Pleased to meet you, he said shaking the man's hand.

What can I do for you, Mr Ferguson? a casual gruffness to his voice.

I got some questions about a deed, Jo Shelby said. But first I have to tell you, I don't have much money. He'd had thirty minutes in the lobby to mull over what he'd say first and decided not to waste any more time, his or the lawyer's.

We'll just call this an initial consultation, *pro bono,* he said.

Pro what?

It's Latin. Means I'm not charging you, Mr Darden said. Come on back. He motioned with his hand and Jo Shelby followed the aging attorney down a narrow hallway lined with framed photographs into a large musty room surrounded by calf-bound books and smelled of dust and old paper, of deep woods.

We can sit here in the library, Mr Darden said. My office is too cluttered, getting ready to go to trial.

I know about trials.

Mr Darden motioned to a leatherback chair at the end of a long polished table. Jo Shelby pulled the chair out and took a seat and the attorney did likewise across from him.

Say you know about trials, Mr Darden said, his eyebrows arching above his wire-frame glasses.

Jo Shelby told him about the charges filed against him for the slaying of Luke Clister, a man of his own color, of the trial and conviction and time served afterward and his eventual release on August 9 of last year when Junior Washington, a Negro, confessed to the crime after being apprehended and taken into custody for another slaying long on the books.

I remember that trial, Mr Darden said. Dudley Trotter from Indianola defended you.

Yessir. Court-appointed.

Court-appointed or not, Dudley's a good attorney. What evidence did the prosecution have?

Circumstantial, he said then went on to tell him how he'd been to the picture show and stopped by Wang's grocery to get a bottle of pop and a candy bar before heading home and heard something in the alley that ran between the picture show and the chinaman's store. How he stepped into something wet he thought was water and bent down to check on a man he thought was just drunk and when he reached out to steady himself his hand came down on a lead pipe. What I stepped in wasn't water, he said.

And your fingerprints were all over that pipe, the attorney said gravely.

Yes sir.

And you didn't have an alibi.

Yes sir. I mean no sir, I didn't.

You called the ambulance?

No sir. I went inside the store and told Mr Wang to call one, then I went back out and tried to help the man in his suffering, wait for the ambulance so I could direct em to him.

You didn't call the police?

No sir. Didn't think to. All I wanted to do was get the man help. Mr Darden, sir, if you don't mind my saying, you're makin me feel like I'm on that witness stand again.

I'm sorry, Mr Ferguson. Habit of the trade. I do have one more question, though.

Yes sir?

What motive did they convict you on?

Robbery.

Robbery?

The next day was my mama's birthday. I'd been working some for my daddy, saving up to get her a nice electric sewing machine. She loved to sew. Made most of our clothes. Had my eye on this new-fangled Singer that could do all kinds of things, including zig-zaging. By the time I got to town, Western Auto had already closed.

So you were walking around with—

With over a hundred dollars in my pocket and the dead man's wife said on the witness stand that's about how much he had when he left home that night.

Silence stretched in the small library. Only the sounds of the secretary pecking away on a typewriter down the hall. Mr Darden lowered his head and looked at Jo Shelby over the tops of his glasses. Mr Ferguson, you do put a different twist to the meaning of the word circumstantial.

Maybe so. One thing's for sure though.

What's that?

The help that could've come to my rescue never came.

There's more to this story, Mr Darden said, leaning across the table toward him.

Yessir. A lot more.

I see. Well, we might as well get down to business. He pulled a gold pen from his inside coat pocket, made a swirl in the air and jotted something on a yellow pad. What's this about a deed?

That's the rest of the story. It's long, might take a while.

Think you can tell it in an hour?

Yessir.

Very well, proceed, and he chopped the air with his hand like he might have been signaling the start of a race.

He began when he got out of prison with no family to turn to and found his great-great-great-grandmama's letters in the family trunk, the only worldly possession left to him then told how he took off to Mexico because the letters more than hinted he still had family somewhere in that country. He told how they got to be there in the first place, that his great-great-great-grandfather Colonel Calvin T. Ferguson, rather than be tried by Yankees when Lee surrendered at Appomattox, took his family and joined General

J. O. Shelby's army (for whom he was named, he threw in) in its march to Mexico to set up another Confederacy so the South could rise again. He backed up to explain that one of the Colonel's sons, Foster, chose to stay with the land, then he moved forward to 1875, to the burning of the house and subsequent loss of both the ruined house and the land by Foster in a poker or crap game, but that it wasn't his to lose because the old man, Colonel Calvin T., was still alive and well in Mexico at the time.

He paused and cleared his throat and Mr Darden called for his secretary to bring glasses and a pitcher of iced water.

A rich Yankee named Marshall, Jo Shelby continued, carpetbagger or scalawag or both, was the one who got the land, then in 1913 he sold it to a Patrick, at least that's what my daddy said and—

Hold on a second, Mr Darden said, raising a finger. Did you say Patrick?

Yessir. Anything wrong?

No sir. Not yet. Go on.

Anyway it's been in their family's name ever since. But my family's lived on it ever since, too. Foster and his wife Esther stayed on as tenants which was their only choice or starve. This Marshall fellow made him foreman because he didn't know a middlebuster from a harrow. Then when Foster died, his son, Nathan Bedford Ferguson, took his place, then he died and my granddaddy, Nathan Foster, took over and so on right down to my daddy who was the foreman, too. That is till he was killed with my mama in a car wreck when I was in prison. That's pretty much it, the way my mama and daddy passed it on to me. Except for one more thing I almost forgot.

By all means don't leave anything out, Mr Darden said. His eyes were intent, his fingertips steepled beneath his chin.

He went on to tell him about his father's trips to the Sunflower County Court house to investigate, how he got the runaround every time, as if there was a big secret, big enough somebody was being paid to keep.

Mr Darden removed his glasses, leaned across the table and looked at him thoughtfully. Where are the letters now?

I've got two of them in this knapsack. He pulled it from the floor and laid it on the table. I took them with me to Mexico, to show for proof. The

Patricks have the rest, said they'd keep them for me till I got back, along with my family's trunk and the artifacts in it.

Wait a minute, Mr Darden said, narrowing his eyes at the ceiling, a disturbed look on his face. This is the second time you've made reference to the Patrick name. Is this Jack Hurley Patrick?

Yessir.

And you're coming back here to file a suit against Jack Hurley Patrick and he's keeping your things for you?

Yessir. He doesn't know about the suit, if it even goes that far, which is why I'm here. I'm going to get my things first. You know him?

The attorney rolled his eyes. Yessir. Afraid I do.

Afraid?

Mr Darden grinned tightly, then snickered through his nose. No, not afraid in the fearful sense of the word. It's just that there's another story about as long as yours.

The hour's not over.

It would take a lot longer than any hour. I know Jack Hurley Patrick, known him all his life. Had to sue him a couple of times myself.

That a fact? What over, if I might ask?

Boundary disputes.

The two men looked silently at each other, the uttered irony conveying the rest.

Well, this is more than a boundary dispute, Jo Shelby said. That land still belongs in my family's name.

The attorney's smile melted into a thin serious line. If your great-great-grandfather Foster lost it in a poker or crap game, whichever, to this Marshall fellow and didn't deliver a deed, I'm just not sure how that would shake out. That's a very gray area.

That's why I'm here. I aim to make it black and white.

So this trip to Mexico you took, Mr Darden said, it was more than just a search for your family, albeit on another branch of your family tree.

No sir, at the time that's all it was. I'd gotten out of prison, didn't have anybody, not family anyway. I'd pretty much decided the other was a lost cause, about as lost as the reason those Confederates went to Mexico. Then I saw the tombstone. That was when it hit me.

Tombstone?

Yessir. I gotta back up. He recapitulated his long trip to Mexico, how by hitchhiking and various conveyances he met a priest in Michapa and a lady in Cuernavaca, who both knew his great-great grandparents on the Mexican side of the family, then how he found one Senora Carlita Navarro Cruze Mondaca, his last living relative at the Hacienda Tierra de la Puenta south of Cuernavaca.

How were you sure she was related to you? Mr Darden said.

Because ... . He reached into his knapsack and pulled out an official-looking document and laid it onto the table in front of the attorney. Because it's all right there, in these documents from the Registro in Cuernavaca. He went on to explain how the documents proved the lineage from Carolina Suzanna Ferguson, his great-great grandmother, on down to Carlita Navarro Cruze Moncada, their birth dates and marriage dates, that they were all probable heirs to a great hacienda north of the border if ever there was found the will of one Calvin T. Ferguson wherein he bequeathed at least a portion to his daughter, Carolina Suzanna, who married Fernando Alfonzo Cruse Linares, the son of a wealthy Mexican don.

I also got this, Jo Shelby continued, reaching once more into the knapsack and retrieving a small spiral notebook. Every thing I did and saw, I wrote down, drew some pictures of places, too. He told how, with the help of people along the way, he eventually found the Hacienda Michopa, or what was left of it, a burned-out, crumbling adobe shell of a once great house with magnificent walls and gardens and fountains, that it really did exist at one time and his great-great-great grandparents really did live there, and die there. He told how he found the church where they were buried, what the dates on the blackened slab markers said, that Caroline B. died 1881 and the Colonel in 1882, that they were both alive, long after 1875 and the crap or poker game, whatever it was, and with that brought his hand down onto the table with a clap of finality.

The old attorney just sat there, staring at him as though transfixed, as though hearing and seeing were not believing.

You mean to tell me, Mr Ferguson, that your great-grandparents of long ago just up and left, went to Mexico with General Shelby and there has been no contact with the family since then?

Yessir. It tells why in the letters. They were afraid of being hunted down. Once that Indian, Juarez was his name, got back into power—he and Mr Lincoln were friends—they were afraid the Mexicans would arrest them and send them home where my granddaddy would be tried. That's what they thought. So they were afraid to write anymore, afraid their letters would be intercepted. Foster was too busy trying to just hang onto the place. He didn't know where to send a letter even if he wrote one. A thousand miles is a long way. Guess it just gets longer over time. That's it, Mr Darden, sir. I don't have a watch, but don't think I took up the hour.

Mr Darden stretched out his arm and looked at his wristwatch. No sir, Mr Ferguson, you did mighty fine in less than an hour, and I'm sensing you left out a lot at that.

Yessir. I did. Wanted to get down to the lick log.

Well, you sure enough did that, he chuckled. Young man you've presented one helluva situation, taking us places the law's rarely been.

I've been there, too.

He nodded. I reckon you have. But I'm speaking legally. You see all these books surrounding us? He waved a hand around the room.

Yessir.

There's not one single case, I know of, in any of these books for the situation you have presented. He massaged his temples with his fingers, then propped them beneath his chin again. You're talking about something that happened a long time ago. It's going to be practically impossible to reconstruct a factual sequence that will withstand that passage of time. There are so many angles. First of all, did the colonel have a will? Because if he did, and it was probated, it would probably be of record. Secondly, and more importantly, was the courthouse even in existence back then? Some were burned after the Civil War, to get rid of the tax records. I wonder if there are even records dating back that far. One thing you do have going in your favor is that a gambling debt is not enforceable by law. Foster delivering a deed is one thing. And there might be a record of that. But losing the property outright in a crap game. That's a horse of a different color. Two things, however, are not in your favor. Adverse possession and statute of limitation.

What's that mean?

Adverse possession is when someone else stakes a claim illegally on your property. If I have a piece of land and you build a fence over on my property and I've got clear title but don't say anything about it, don't protest, don't say look a here Ferguson I'm getting me a lawyer and sue you, get some record of it, then after ten years—you've had the fence there and you've been occupying the land, farming it, planting peach trees on it, whatever—after ten years it's yours. I've given up my right to it, acquiesced. This is a statute, a statute is a law, dating back to 1848, and revised in 1942, section 711 of the Mississippi Code. If a person lives on a piece of property, uses it, stays there and doesn't leave it for ten years, then it's his. The ten years gives him good title, color of title it's called, as long as no one has exercised rightful claim to the property. Ten years is the statute of limitation. You understand?

Yessir. Think I do. You said something about a will. What if there was one?

Oh yes. I did at that. Now if the colonel had a will, even if it was written in his own hand and not witnessed, and that will was probated, that would mean the court established it was valid. In other words, there'd be a record of it. If that were the case, then this Foster may not have had the right to transfer the property title, if in fact that happened.

What if there was a will but it wasn't probated, wasn't probated because he took it with him. Or if he didn't take it with him, he left it behind with somebody for safekeeping and that somebody, maybe my great-great-granddaddy Foster, decided not to probate it because it wouldn't let him pay off his gamblin debt if he did. In other words, my granddaddy Foster struck a deal with this Marshall feller that they'd agree to forget about the will if Foster could stay on the place and work and feed his family and keep a roof over their heads, which is what happened.

If that's the case, and you can come up with a will that hadn't been probated, you might just be in luck.

But you said something bout ten years being all the time allowed and we've already run out of that, six or seven times that.

That ten years was a statute of limitation having to do with rightful claim to property. Didn't have anything to do with wills. In the state of Mississippi there is no statute of limitations on the probate of a will. I've heard of wills probated all the way back to the Civil War. If you came up with a copy of the colonel's will, written in his own hand or otherwise, and it was not probated, it could just turn this situation on its head.

That's what I aim to do. Can you help me?

Mr Darden leaned back and smiled. It's not that simple, Mr Ferguson, but I like your spunk. Let me think about it. I'll need to check the records at the courthouse, try and locate the deed, see if it's still there, check its history, the tax records. See if there's a probated will somewhere down there in the books.

If it's all the same to you, Mr Darden, sir, I'd like to do some of that checking myself.

Mr Darden looked at him circumspectly. You are one determined young man, Mr Ferguson. You're about to get into a part of the law you've never seen. But you go ahead, see what you come up with. I can come behind you and fill in the rest, especially the tax records, to see if this man Marshall paid taxes on the land. That could make it even trickier.

That reminds me. There's something I hadn't told you.

I can't believe there'd be more.

Back there when I was telling you about my arrest and the help that never came and you said there's more to this story.

Mr Darden gave a slight nod.

Well, sir, this is the *more* I didn't tell.

Mr Darden leaned back again in his chair and twirled a finger in the air. Go on, he said.

He told him about his relationship with Jack Patrick's only daughter, Athen, how they'd grown close over the years, too close to suit her daddy and mama, the reason her daddy not only gave the sheriff permission to come on his property but acted as though he welcomed the intrusion, even accompanied him down to the house with two gun-toting deputies walking

stride for stride beside him, as if the sheriff needed any more help appre-
hending an eighteen-year-old just out of high school. He told how he was
interrogated on his own front porch in front of his mama and daddy and Mr
Pat and told the truth but it didn't matter because his fingerprints were on
the weapon and he didn't have an alibi and there were no other suspects.
Then the sheriff handcuffed him and Mr Pat allowed it because he didn't,
wouldn't, couldn't ever allow his daughter dating hired help. That's why
help never came, he said, and stopped.

I don't think you're through, Mr Darden said.

No sir. I'm not.

You still care about her?

That's one of the reasons I came back.

And she still cares for you?

She did when I left.

You say that with some question in your voice, Mr Darden said.

She gave me her phone number and address. I wrote her one letter.

That's all?

It's hard to write when you're moving around all the time. She doesn't
even know if I'm alive. He paused and looked down, then back up into the
attorney's eyes. She's real pretty.

Yes. I know. She's quite beautiful. I guess you won't know if she still
cares unless you see her again.

That's the tricky part. I think you can figure it from there. When she
learns about this lawsuit, if you'll excuse my French, the shit's gonna hit the
fan.

Mr Darden chuckled then his face slipped back into its serious mode.
Maybe. Maybe not.

What do you mean maybe not?

Just that. Street talk is she's not like them, her mama and daddy. Or her
brothers for that matter. Got a mind of her own.

I wouldn't know. I was only with her a few hours before I took off for
Mexico.

I'd say you've got some catching up to do.

I may be too far behind.

You started out behind when you got out of prison. I'd say you've covered a good country mile in record time and short order.

Two countries, to be more accurate.

That you have.

I do plan to see her. Didn't come all the way back not to. I've just got to figure how to do it.

Based on the young man I've come to know in only one hour, I believe you will.

I think that's all my story, Jo Shelby said. If I said any more I'd be making it up. I'd be mighty proud to have your help, that is if I can afford it, which is the part we hadn't talked about yet.

I'll tell you what young fellow.

Ferguson. Jo Shelby Ferguson.

My apologies. Mr Ferguson. Don't know if I can help you with the young lady. You're on your own there. But you've impressed me with such a compelling argument about the land, not to mention the story along with it, I'll be happy to help you with the title issue. If you come out empty handed, you don't owe me anything. If it turns out you've got a case, and we convince the court you have a case, you owe me twenty-five percent of your share of the plantation's first year's net profit after the court judgment. Fair enough?

Fair enough. But I want to think about the money part.

You think it's too much?

No sir. Might not be enough. I just want what's fair. For everybody.

Mr Darden called his secretary back to the room, dictated an agreement to her, which she quickly typed and he laid on the table for Jo Shelby to sign.

Jo Shelby took the pen, looked a long time at the single sheet, put the pen down.

Something wrong? Mr Darden said.

No sir. Nothing wrong. I just don't make deals this fast. Almost gave up a gun once that might've saved my life because I was in a hurry to make a deal. Everything looks okay. I want to sleep on it.

Very well. I'll leave it with Mary Lou at the front desk. If you come in and I'm not here, she'll have it for you to sign.

They shook hands again.

Jo Shelby turned and was about to leave, then turned back around. I got one question.

Yes, sir?

Mr Darden, why is it you're so willing to help me? I'm sure you've got bigger cases where you'll make more money?

The old attorney thought a moment then crooked a finger in the air and motioned for Jo Shelby to follow him. They left the library, walked a short distance down the hallway and turned into an office. Mr Darden had said he was getting ready for a trial but by the looks of his office, one had already come and gone, Jo Shelby thought. Like a tornado comes and goes.

On one wall by itself hung a large picture of Lee surrendering to Grant at Appomattox, and on the one adjacent several framed documents, by the large gold seals on them, awards of some kind. But it was to the wall behind the cluttered desk Mr Darden proceeded, stepping over piles of paper, some top-heavy and near collapse and others already fallen and splayed onto the floor so if a shoe hit them just right the body attached to it would be on the floor with them. But the old attorney negotiated deftly and agilely through the paper jungle as though it was a daily memorized trek until he stood beside a large framed document, discolored with age, nothing on it except what appeared to be a grid-work of thin brown lines.

That's the plat of my family's property, Mr Darden said, facing Jo Shelby and pointing over his shoulder, then turning to gaze solemnly upon it. It's not the original, of course. That's in the county court house. I know it's there because its history, he turned back around, doesn't go back nearly as far as yours. That's several thousand acres, good rich Delta soil, he said, thumping the glass covering.

You still got it? Jo Shelby said.

Almost.

Almost?

This is the story, Mr Darden began. My family owned all this land, procured it much the way yours did, adding a little here, a little there, beating back the wilderness. Then in the thirties the depression came. Times were tough. My daddy's mules died, both of them, some kind of strange disease, strange still to this day. He had to have mules or he couldn't plant. People were mean in those days, lean and hungry mean. There was this one planter up the road who said he'd give my daddy a couple of mules.

Just give em to him? Jo Shelby interrupted.

Not give. That was the catch. He'd trade them to him for all this, he said, tracing the largest sector of the plat, which was most of it, with his finger.

Your daddy traded all that land for two mules. Well I'll be damn.

That's right. Mules were hard to come by, worth their weight in gold. Like I said, people were lean and mean in those days.

You said that you almost had it all back, Jo Shelby said.

That's right. I promised my father on his deathbed I would do everything in my power to recover that land. He told me to do it by hook or by crook but I didn't want to be like the people who practically stole it from him, which may have been one of the reasons I went to law school and became a lawyer. So, little by little I've been buying back the land.

And the man's willing to sell it back to you?

At his price, he is.

What's the man's name?

Mr Darden tipped his head forward and leveled his eyes at Jo Shelby over the top rim of his glasses. Jack Hurley Patrick.

They walked back down the hall and into the small lobby where Mary Lou was still pecking away on the typewriter. Mr Darden walked him to the door and opened it for him. Jo Shelby turned back to him before stepping into the open frame. I got one more question.

You can ask as many as you want.

No sir. Just this one, for right now, will do. Who won those two cases, the ones where you sued Mr Pat?

He won one and I won one.

I'd say it was bout time to get a leg up.

Mr Darden smiled and nodded. Speaking of which, I have a suggestion after all regarding that gal, Athens's her name I believe.

Yessir.

Don't take offense, Mr Ferguson, but I think you might be a leg up yourself if you got those front teeth fixed.

No offense taken. I've already looked into that then he put his hat back on, tipped it at the young lady typing and stepped from the office onto the sidewalk.

He walked back to the dentist's office and went in.

The car was an old rattle-trap beat-up Ford and the man driving it as worn and damaged in years. A brown-speckled goiter ballooned jelly-like from his neck like a fungus growth from the limb of an oak and when he leaned his head out the window, his face looked like a punching bag with part of the air let out. He squinted so his eyes were near shut and his voice rattled from deep in his chest like it was all he could do to breathe. But Jo Shelby had been standing there on the side of the road for over two hours and with the afternoon wearing on, this might be his last chance for a ride north.

He walked to the passenger side to get in and the man told him to climb through the window, that the door wouldn't open. Jo Shelby leveraged himself in feet-first, dragging his knapsack in behind him, then the odor hit him. He wondered how much the man had had to drink, if he should quickly say thanks but no thanks and slide back out the way he came in but the car was already lurching forward and careening up the highway. Rome was only eleven miles away, but by the sound of the knocking in the engine and fender slapping against the fender-well and another sound he could not discern, he wondered which would happen first, the car self-destructing by the sheer combined forces of movement and gravity or a head-on collision. He gripped his knapsack in front of his chest. The car weaved a short distance then straightened its course between shoulder and centerline. The rattling and knocking continued but the old man seemed to find a groove, like it takes some things a while to warm up once they stop or shut down.

Within a few miles the towers of the penitentiary came into view. As they neared its entrance, he asked the man if he could slow down.

This aint no limousine, the man said, his speech slurring slightly over protruding lips, the least movement of his head causing the globular mass on his neck to bounce and roll. Jo Shelby tried not to look at it but it was almost all you could see of the man from the shoulders up.

The man eased his foot off the accelerator. You got some reason you want me to slow down? the man said, his eyes cutting suspiciously on his passenger.

He had a reason but not one he wanted to share. On second thought, guess not, he said.

The man's foot pressed down and the car speeded up.

Where you headed to in Rome? the old man said.

Going to the Stevens' place, his eyes fixed on the open road.

Bo Stevens, down past the Patrick place?

Yessir.

I'm going to Clarksdale. It's on my way. Don't mind dropping you off there.

That'd be mighty kind of you, he said.

Sure nough, the man said, his head bobbing over the wheel, the bag on his neck bouncing with it.

The Stevens had always been friendly to him and his family. They'd gone to the same Methodist Church in Rome. Miss Floy and his mama worked on the same church committees. When his mama ran out of flour or milk or needed an extra egg, it was Miss Floy Jo Shelby rode down and borrowed them from, not Miss Pat fifty steps away. His father and Mr Bo visited often. The two properties adjoined each other and it wasn't out of the ordinary for his daddy to direct the colored workers on Patrick tractors across the property line to help Mr Bo when he was short of help. The two men hunted together, played chess, drank a beer or two together every once in a while. Often Jo Shelby was with them, particularly when they rode horses. Mr Bo had come to see him in prison a number of times. Mr Pat's shadow never darkened the front gate.

The Stevens were planters, but not like the Patricks. They didn't own the acreage the Patricks owned and didn't live in a mansion. They didn't drive Cadillacs and go to the Ruleville Club every Saturday night. They didn't put on airs or wear fancy clothes, have a swimming pool or tennis court in their back yard. They weren't trying to keep up with anybody, or get ahead either, which was why they weren't in hock to the bank, his daddy once told him. They had a son and a daughter, both grown and married.

One lived in Atlanta and the other Nashville. Good folks. That was what his daddy and mama called them. Good folks pretty much said it all.

Past the city limits sign, they turned left off the main highway onto the narrow macadam that dog-legged through the small cluster of houses and stores that was Rome, Mississippi, past Mr J. W. Pope's mercantile store where the large sign over the awning said POPE OF ROME. Jo Shelby chuckled to himself at the story as it had come down to him, how three Catholic nuns stopped one day objecting to the sign and how Mr J. W. told them his name was Pope and the only one in the town with the name so why shouldn't he be THE Pope of Rome.

They approached the brick pillars with the white wrought-iron arch that said PATRICK.

Mind slowing down just a bit, Jo Shelby said.

Agin? the man whined.

Don't have to stop. Just slow down while we go past the Patrick place.

They friends of yours, too?

Kind of. He wasn't ready to see her yet, the speech he was going to give still unborn. She might be there and she might not. It was Saturday. It was early spring and not football season, which meant kids coming home on weekends to get their clothes washed and a home cooked meal and a little extra spending money. She just might be. He decided not to press his luck. He could see her and get the trunk and letters later, all that depending on whether or not Mr Bo could give him work.

The man slowed the car. Jo Shelby set his face and prepared his eyes, then drove his vision up the pecan-lined drive as they sailed past the arched opening, to glimpse what he could, if there was any sign of her. But all he could see was a flash of the white-columned house through the barred trees, a Cadillac parked in front and a flicker of something red in the parking area to the side of the house, something that might have been a car and might not have been. He thought again of stopping, then not stopping, stopping, then not, as if red and green were blinking off and on behind his eyes, then decided the color he needed to see was green and they rode on.

The Stevens lived in a rambling single-story ranch-style house set just off the road behind a thick green wall of privy hedge. Adjacent the house was a two-story garage and behind that a short distance the barn, additional out buildings and a long open shed for the farm equipment.

The man didn't turn the car into the drive through the hedge but stopped and let Jo Shelby out on the side of the road.

I'm much obliged, mister, Jo Shelby said. Hope you make it all right to Clarksdale. He almost said in one piece, but it seemed too late for that. He just hoped he made it.

Don't mention it, the man slurred with a backward flip of an unsteady hand, then revved the engine with a foot numbed to the power beneath it as the tires made a slight squeal on the pavement and the vehicle lurched forward.

Jo Shelby stood and watched as the ruined contraption bucked away, its carriage swinging precariously low, then glimpsed the cause of the other noise he couldn't make out. The exhaust pipe hanging down, sparking against the asphalt. He wondered about that kind of life and all that came to mind was wrecked. A life born wrecked and living wrecked and dying wrecked and he contemplated that barren despairing existence, how it could be living in a world without hope, without life ever being any different. But his thinking could not plumb that depth.

He climbed the two steps to the only door he'd ever passed through at the Stevens, one that served as both front and back door because that was the Stevens. They didn't need but one door.

He knocked twice. He waited a while, raised a fist to knock again and Miss Floy came to the door. Her name was Florence as in Florence Nightingale, his mother had told him, but Miss Floy was all he'd ever known.

Jo Shelby Ferguson, she said with wide eyes, smiling grandly, her hands coming together in a single clap. Heaven's sakes? She was a small woman, much like his mother. She had a small round face, short curly hair, bright eyes and a smile that never quit, like his mother. She was one of those fine ladies of the South that give it its good name. Like his mother.

Afternoon, Miss Floy he said.

My lands, and look at that mouth, she said, leaning in close and scrutinizing the gap in his teeth. How did that happen?

It's a long story, he said, matching her smile with a toothless grin. But it's a good one.

Come on in. Bo's in the den. He'll be tickled to see you. We want to hear all about it, she said holding the screen door open for him.

He bent over to set his knapsack on the stoop.

Bring your bag in with you, she said.

He removed his hat, dusted it against his leg then followed her through the doorway into the house.

She led him through the kitchen into the den, a moderate sized room of pine paneling, fireplace at one end, sofa and chairs spread evenly in a semicircle around it and a large round coffee table covered with magazines and newspapers. Some colorful rugs of various shapes and sizes covered a hardwood floor and a couple of family portraits hung on one wall next to a glass encasement of Mr Bo's antique gun collection.

Look what just appeared on our doorstep, Miss Floy said.

Mr Bo was sitting in one of the leather chairs reading a newspaper, his sock feet propped up on an ottoman. Jo Shelby saw first the bald head then the big jolly, rosy-cheeked face as the paper came down.

Well, I'll be a son of a gun, he said with a smile that stretched to his gold-capped molars. He swung his legs off the ottoman and propelled himself upward from the chair.

Jo Shelby how in the world are you?

Jo Shelby shook his hand. I'm still in it.

I'll say. Glad to see you made it back.

We had no idea what happened to you, Miss Floy said. First, we read in the Drew paper where you had been released from prison, then heard that you'd gone to Mexico, of all places.

How'd you hear that?

Hilda Patrick told her at church, Mr Bo said.

Jo Shelby had forgotten the woman had another name. He'd always called her Miss Pat.

Have a seat. Take a load off. We want to hear all about your journey, Mr
Bo said.

Well, give him a chance to rest, Miss Floy said. He's been days on the
road to get here, I'm sure. You must be thirsty.

Yessum. Some water'd be nice.

If he'd been at the Patricks,' Miss Pat would have called for Sissy, their
maid, to bring him a glass of iced water. But it wasn't the Patricks' and the
Stevens didn't have a maid and those thoughts brought a certain comfort.
Except he missed Sissy. She lived down the road between the Stevens and
Patricks and he'd surely have to go by and see her.

Miss Floy stepped up into the kitchen.

Jo Shelby, we can't say enough in way of condolences about your mama
and daddy and granddaddy, Mr Bo said.

Your comin to the prison to see me was enough, Jo Shelby said.

I couldn't believe they wouldn't let you out for the funeral, your own
family's of all things. I tried, talked to the warden. But he said rules were
rules, that you'd hit a guard and if he broke one rule for you, the breaking
wouldn't stop and he'd hear about it all the way from the governor's office
on down.

That's what he said?

Yep. That's what he said, what he told everybody else, too.

He got part of it right. But I never hit a guard. One said it was a fine day
and I said it wasn't and he hit me with the butt of his gun.

I'll say. That's a cruel world down there.

It's not a world. It's hell.

From the kitchen sounds of ice-cubes being knocked out of a tray into a
glass, then water running.

Guess it is at that, Mr Bo said.

Miss Floy returned and handed him a tumbler of water filled to the top
with ice, a napkin wrapped around it. Sit down for heaven's sakes, she said,
settling into a chair next to Mr Bo.

He sat in a leather wingback near the fireplace and began his story. He
told them of his travels by boat and tanker to Brownsville, the incident with
the gun and his incarceration in the Mexican prison in Matamoros, the

beatings and brush with death, of his new friend Ramon, how he got him out of prison and how all that was accomplished within a large and mysterious network of politics and intrigue he never fully understood. He told of his brief stay with Ramon's wife in Monterrey, the help she afforded him, then of their daughter, Carmen, in Mexico City, of his time with her and how she helped him research his family in the University library. He could have said more about Carmen but figured he'd said too much already.

He reached into his knapsack on the floor beside him and removed the large map of Mexico Athen had given to him before his departure. He left his chair and got on his knees, spread the map onto the floor, traced his journey from Monterrey to Mexico City then to Cuernavaca. Mr Bo and Miss Floy leaned forward from their chairs, their eyes steadily focused on his moving finger. He painted the land as he went, its patchwork of towering mountains, vast and desolate plateaus, rich and fruitful plains, kind and benevolent people, scratching up from his meager vocabulary the most fitting words to describe all that was good and grand and magnificent about this land that in every way had a heart bigger than the sun. The discovery of La Hacienda Tierra del Puenta he covered in greater detail, explaining the information obtained from The Registry in Cuernavaca, the circuitous route that brought him to the valley and the hacienda, the near hanging by the foreman there, then stopped with his meeting of Senora Carlita Navarro Cruz Moncada, his lost relative from another time, another family tree.

She was the one who stopped the hanging, he said. I'm not sure which she is, aunt or cousin. She read these letters. He reached again into his knapsack and retrieved the creased and frayed pages, passing one set to Mr Bo, the other to Miss Floy. All I know is we're kin, he said. And that was why I went.

He stopped and moved back into his chair, took a long drink from the tumbler.

So that was where you got your teeth knocked out, Miss Floy said before beginning the letter he'd given to her. Not in prison.

Yessum. He said nothing else and gave them time to read the letters.

Mr Bo finished with his letter and swapped with Miss Floy and the two continued reading.

Mr Bo collected the pages of the letter he was reading, laid them on his ottoman then looked seriously at him. Jo Shelby, now don't misunderstand me. We are mighty glad to see you. Your family was like family to us. Your daddy may have been the best friend I had. But what I don't understand is why you went all the way to Mexico to find your family, found em, what was left of em, then left as soon as you found em, along with a good job in a place as grand as you say it is and came back here to Mississippi, to Rome of all places, where you've got nothing.

Miss Floy stopped reading and looked up, as if the question came from her, as well. He took another long drink from his glass, set it onto the polished table beside him, careful to place it on the napkin Miss Floy had provided. The room grew quiet.

Let's just say I've got some unfinished business. If I said more than that, we'd be here till midnight.

We stay up late, Miss Floy said.

Mr Bo shot her a look of advisement.

But we don't have to know right this minute, she said quickly. Might not be any of our business anyway.

I would like to know about that gun, Mr Bo said. You say you found it in a trunk left by your folks?

Miss Floy resumed reading.

Yessir. That was all they left. With me being in prison and not expected out for another fifteen years or so, if that, the Patricks gave everything away to charities and the needy, said my mama would have wanted it that way, which she would. Every thing except some family memories, pictures, old stuff from the War Between the States.

What kind of gun was it? Mr Bo said.

Navy Colt, lever-action. It's real old.

I'll say, Mr Bo said. That's some artifact. Navy Colts are hard to come by. He pointed at his collection on the wall. Been looking for one in good condition for some time. One that doesn't cost an arm and a leg.

It almost cost me every bit that, Jo Shelby said. Got me in prison and got me out.

What happened to it? Miss Floy said, impressing Jo Shelby with her ability to read and listen at the same time.

Pawned it.

Pawned it? Mr Bo said. How could you do that after all it had gotten you through?

I can have it back if I pay the man a hundred dollars within six months of when I made the deal. I had to do something. I was broke. Comes a time a man has to decide between today and tomorrow and the gun didn't seem to have much promise for tomorrow cept the money I got for it which got me to the tomorrow that counted.

You plan to go back and get it? Mr Bo said.

Not sure. Prob'ly not. I got a friend down there who can get it for me, and he mentioned Carmen again. As soon as I can make a hundred dollars and send it to her.

Miss Floy looked up from her letter again, looked at Mr Bo who was looking at her. You've mentioned this Carmen a few times. Sounds like she might be more than just a friend.

Mr Bo shot her another hard look.

A real good friend, that's all, Jo Shelby said, feeling the blood rise into his cheeks. He wanted to say something else, but decided he'd said enough.

Floy, for cryin out loud, leave the boy alone, Mr Bo said angrily.

Sorry, she said sheepishly. That's just the way mamas think, and she continued reading the letter she was holding.

What are your plans? Mr Bo said, one eyebrow raised above the other. You looking for work?

Yessir. That and a place to stay. He wished he hadn't said it the way he did, like it was a request from the needy.

Miss Floy opened her mouth to say something and Mr Bo raised his hand to stop her. Got a proposition for you, he said.

Yessir? Jo Shelby said.

Farming's gotten more complicated than it used to be, a lot more since you've been away. The government's gotten into it. There are price supports and quotas and allotments on cotton. The price supports have helped and the mechanical pickers are doing about half the work now. We, along with others, are planting soybeans and combining those with some success. But it seems you can't have the good without the bad. Because more machines are doing more of the work, the nigras are going North, to Chicago and other places where they can make more money and the good white workers are moving into the towns, getting factory jobs, steady work.

Factories?

I keep forgetting you've been out of commission a while, Mr Bo said. Baxter Laboratories started up in Cleveland in 1949. There's a broomhandle factory in Belzoni. Alexander Smith Company in Greenville and Stoutwear in Clarksdale. The Delta Council has been calling for more industry in the past few years. They say the Delta's lagging behind the rest of the state. They need the industry—

What Bo is trying to tell you, Miss Floy spoke up, is that we could use your help here. He's been short-handed for a couple years now.

We've got a little apartment over the garage, Mr Bo said. The last foreman we had used it then he got married and moved on. It's been vacant, nothing fancy, could use a little work, but you could stay there. I'd pay you the going rate.

That'd be mighty generous of you.

I tried to get your daddy to come and work for me, but he had other ideas.

Yessir, Jo Shelby said. I know about those.

The two men looked at each other, their eyes telegraphing understanding.

I don't know how Jack Hurley's getting along without him, Mr Bo said. He's got a new man, name's Ligon. But he's not half the man your daddy was.

Miss Floy finished the second letter and laid it in her lap. Those are quite some letters. It's a miracle they're still around.

Hoping some of that miracle might rub off, Jo Shelby said.

It's just about suppertime, she said. You will stay and eat with us.

If I won't be any trouble.

You'd be in trouble if you didn't, she said smiling.

Bo, you show him the apartment while I get supper ready. She pointed at his knapsack. Is that all you've got?

It's all I got with me. The trunk I was telling you about is at the Patricks', along with the rest of the letters.

You can borrow my pickup tomorrow and get those, Mr Bo said. Let's go look at your new home.

The apartment was one room with an adjoining bath. It was small and had a musty, mildew smell, but it was clean. There was an old brass bed and a nightstand, a small lamp on a white doily on the nightstand, yellow and brown-striped curtains over the two windows that faced east and west. Along the south wall was a short counter with a sink and draining board. A small white-enameled refrigerator chipped around the edges stood in the corner beside the cabinet. Beneath the east window across from the bed was a large oscillating fan.

Dishes and flatware are in the drawer under the draining board, Mr Bo said. There's detergent and cleaning supplies in the cabinet under the sink. They haven't been used in a while, but they'll do the job. He opened the door to show him then shut it. You'll need to get you some groceries. To-morrow's Sunday so the stores'll be closed. You can borrow the truck Monday and run your errands. I can show you around then. You can start work on Tuesday. That'll give you a couple of days to adjust, settle in. I can give you a little advance if you need it.

No sir. Much obliged. I've got enough to get me by. I don't spend much.

Mr Bo smiled. Neither do we, Jo Shelby. Neither do we. He opened his mouth to say something else then closed it, stood there looking at the floor rubbing his chin a while then looked up. You said you came back for some unfinished business. Of course, it's none of my business, but does it have anything to do with Jack Patrick?

Yessir.

I thought so.

How'd you know?

The story you told. Your daddy and me talked a lot. He told me about the land, its history. If I told you all I know, we'd sure enough be here till midnight.

Jo Shelby grinned but said nothing.

Just be careful, Mr Bo said, rolling his brows forward over his eyes. Jack won't be the only one you'll be tangling with.

Athen won't cause any problems. We're friends.

I'm not talking about Athen. I'm talking bout Josh and Jake. Mean as snakes.

The sons. He'd forgotten about them. Both lived on the big place, had houses and families, their own hired help. He thought about kingdoms of long ago he'd read about in school, the word for them. It rhymed with thief but wouldn't come to mind. Thief-dom, something like that. It all began piling up in his head, like a thundercloud building to let go, the simpler politics he'd first considered doubling and trebling, multiplying God only knew how many times over. A network of good ole buddies and debts owed and debts paid and debts due, all of it so thick and deeply interwoven a man would have to have some mythical Jo-blade to hack his way through, much less make sense of it all, find some logic or reason that would untangle it. Yessir, he said. I'll keep a lookout.

Lookout might not help, once you've riled them up, Mr Bo said. What I'm trying to tell you is, you're up against the richest planter in these parts, which means the Delta Council and courthouse crowd, all the way up to the gov'nor. He's one of the governor's colonels. You might think about it. Your dad did, decided it best to keep a roof over his family and food on the table.

What family I've got left is in Mexico. And with all I've been through, food's an afterthought.

Very well, Mr Bo said, looking down and swinging his head back and forth in disbelief. If I can be of any help, you let me know. I won't join a revolution, but I might be able to provide a little groundcover.

Jo Shelby looked around the small apartment. Not bad groundcover for a start.

Mr Bo moved to leave, then stopped at the door. Your backpack looks pretty full. Bet you got clothes that need washing. Leave em it at the bottom of the stairs and Floy'll wash em for you. If there's anything else you need, let us know.

He started down the stairs and Jo Shelby stuck his head in the stairwell and called after him. There is one thing, Mr Bo, he said. Wondered if I could have Thursday afternoon off. I've got a doctor's appointment in Drew, a dentist, he said pointing to the gap in his mouth.

Mr Bo grinned. Consider it done.

And one more thing. You still got the horses?

Yep. All three.

Jo Shelby pulled his pocket watch from his jeans' pocket, positioned it in his palm and glanced down at it. It's almost five o'clock. What time y'all eat supper?

Seven, somewhere's there about.

Mind if I saddle up one and take a ride. Thought I might go down to the cemetery, pay my respects.

Help yourself. You know where everything is. Midnight'll be glad to see you.

Some smells never change, he thought, as he entered the barn bay and the blended odors of uncured hay and dust and cattle, of harness leather and manure washed over him. He walked the length of the barn, past the horses whinnying in their stalls, retrieved a saddle and blanket from the saddle room and carried it back to one of the stalls, as he'd done a hundred times before when he and his daddy rode with Mr Bo.

Midnight looked as handsome as ever, his big eyes gleaming excitedly as Jo Shelby approached him. He leaned over the stall door and stroked the long bone-firm nose and whispered his name, kept whispering it. The horse's lips curled back as if to smile approval and jets of warm air shot through the black bores of his nose as he pushed it closer to him and his hooves champed impatiently on the straw-matted dirt floor.

He took a rope off the hitch rail and opened the stall door, entered and haltered the horse and led him out, then half-hitched the rope to the rail, the horse neighing and straining against the rope. He threw the blanket over him, then worked the saddle up and cradled it into place, pulled up the riding crop and fastened the back cinch. Bridal reins in one hand; he put his boot into the stirrup and with a singular motion propelled himself up into the saddle and felt immediately, surging upward through muscle and sinew and leather, that special power a horse transfers to its rider.

He headed through the barn bay and out the door, the horse nickering with a flourish of excitement as they entered the dusky air that had turned cool and brisk. He flicked the reins and called the horses's name and Midnight engaged a trot down a dirt crop road that led into the fields. Holding the reins loosely just above the saddle horn he rode slightly forward in the saddle, feeling the freedom of other days when he had ridden with his father and remembered what his father had said about the outside of a horse making the inside of a man feel good and understood it now more than ever. At times he gently prodded Midnight with his heels and leaned low over his mane and patted his neck, whispered his name in his ear.

Over the fields the horse loped. The peach orchard came into view, then the outline of the big house and the barn and silo, the out buildings and shed under which were aligned, like machines of war ready for battle, the mechanical cotton pickers that were taking away poor people's jobs. This time of day Mr Pat and Miss Pat were on the patio having late afternoon drinks, a scene of habit unchanged there or anywhere else in the world, he guessed. Wherever there were fine houses and big cars behind gated estates, there were the people who owned them needing a moment to make themselves feel good about it all again, as if the feeling had worn down with age and time and the boredom being rich brings and needed revving up a notch.

He swung his vision left and saw the small house off to itself in a stand of oaks. There was a light on in the front window, where his daddy's chair would have been. His mama would've been sitting across from him on the couch, knitting or reading. He noted, too, the swing set where he had once clambered and swung. The pickup his father had driven parked beneath the trees. There was no other vehicle. Mr Pat provided everything.

Midnight stopped before he could pull on the reins, as if he knew, too, and Jo Shelby sat and looked, an ache climbing his throat. He looked a while longer, wondering who might be at home in the big house, if Athen was there. Then he shook the reins and continued on across the broken rows toward a clump of oak and cedar trees that rose from the land, stood alone against sky and horizon like an island in a chocolate sea, as if it had been there all along, that permanent, that much a part of time itself.

The family graveyard, as word of mouth had passed down over the years, was in the peach orchard behind the house. But when the first Jack Patrick—Big Jack they called him—bought the place in 1913 from the Yankee Marshall, he had the graves dug up and moved to the woods some distance from the house. Then the woods were later cleared for more cotton acreage so what remained now was the patch of earth his eyes were fixed upon, having been plowed around all those years and left undisturbed.

While they were alive, his mother and father had maintained the small cemetery. They kept it mowed, painted the wrought-iron fence black each year and cleaned the gravestones so you could read the names and dates. They put flowers on the graves at Christmas and Easter and birthday and death anniversaries. Each Sunday after church he came with them. They knelt and prayed before walking back to the house for a huge lunch his mother would cook that would make the rest of the day creep by like it had been drugged.

He grew nearer and saw how badly neglected the plot had fallen. The gravestones were hidden by Johnson and broom grass, ragweed and wild onions and an assortment of other unwelcome growth that spiraled wildly through the rusticated and wobbly fence. He stood and assayed the scene and measured the damage of three years, the length of time his parents had been dead. No one had touched it since, he thought, a blade of guilt passing through him. He could've at least stayed and done that before leaving for Mexico.

He dismounted and stepped up and opened the gate. Its unhinged top cried out like a mad owl and the entire fence moved in a drunken wave around the periphery. Had it been dark he might have turned and run. He entered the enclosure, brushing the weeds aside with his foot and in that careful manner located first the gravestones of his parents and read the carved inscriptions: *Here lies Elizabeth Carter Ferguson, Righteousness alone exalted her.* And his father: *Here lies John Mosby Ferguson, a man who loved justice, honored mercy and walked humbly with his God.* He moved then to the others, arranged in the order of their generations, back to Foster and Esther Ferguson, all barely legible, their chiseled inscriptions and names and dates weather-blackened, filmed over with moss and lichen. He stood there amid the waist-high roughage, his eyes cataloging the generations, his mind working the arithmetic, the representation of years. Over six hundred, he estimated, several hundred more if he counted the ones in Mexico and Jefferson Longstreet who died in Cuba with the Rough Riders. When he finished, the sum total surpassed a thousand, not including his own meager twenty-five and he was standing on what remained, what it all came down to, a square-footage of Delta earth near equal the summation of years.

He couldn't stand the sight and began pulling weeds with his bare hands. Most of them snapped above ground level the soil was so dry and he decided to wait and return after a rain. Bring a scrub brush and pan of water, too, to clean the gravestones. He knelt and said a prayer, stayed a while longer, remembering.

He was in that meditative posture, his head down and eyes closed, when Midnight snickered and he heard something behind him, a soft clomping of hoof beats approaching, as if in slow motion, as if with great caution. Then they stopped. He opened his eyes and rose and turned. He cupped a hand over his eyes and squinted and at first all he saw was a horse and rider, a composite silhouette against the setting sun's lateral blaze. Then the horse turned and he saw her face.

Athen!

Jo Shelby Ferguson, she said, her voice as matter-of-fact as if reading his name from a roll call. Her face hard as the flat glare shaping her profile, nothing working there, no light in her eyes. She was astride the palomino he remembered from the rides of their youth. She did not seem glad to see him. She did not seem anything. She was just suddenly there, facing him, his thoughts racing to catch up to the image just dropped from nowhere into his life.

A breeze blew her long hair around her face and she brushed it back with a hand. I thought it might be you, she said in that same flat, inflectionless voice that could be anger or joy, hurt or gladness, one that could go either way, that fell on his ears that uncertain. Then I thought, no, it couldn't be, a wiry edge cutting through her voice. The Jo Shelby I know would've let me know he was coming. He would have at least told me he was back in town.

Well ... I ...

At least that.

He tried to speak but his breathing was in the way.

She walked the horse closer then stopped. She looked more beautiful than he remembered, if that was possible, another reason his speech was throttled back where he swallowed.

That looks like one of Bo Stevens' horses. Why didn't you let me know you were here? her voice climbing now, a whine pitching with hurt.

I've only been here a couple of hours, he finally managed. I stopped at Mr Bo's and Miss Floy's then came on here. I was going to see you next. That was not the truth, but *was* had suddenly become *is*. The truth does have a way, sometimes, of shifting and readjusting with time and circumstance.

Brusquely, she wrapped the reins around the saddle's pommel and dismounted. Why didn't you tell me you were coming? she said, standing beside the horse, one hand still on the pommel, a posture suggesting she might remount and ride on.

I've got an excuse. He forced a weak smile and took a step toward her.

I hope it's a good one, she said, and began walking slowly toward him.

He watched her wide cocky stride, the shape her moving figure cut in the early dark, trim in the tight blue jeans and white blouse she was wearing. He remembered back to when it was no shape, when shape didn't matter and he began walking toward her, his mind working again on his speech.

Her stride quickened and his matched it and then they were running.

The impact almost knocked him down. Her arms were tight around his neck, their bodies trembling together, her breath heavy in his ears, her words whispering over and over, God, it's good to see you, God it's good to see you. She'd knocked his hat off and their heads were pressed together, the aroma of her hair rising sweetly in his memory, one that had carried him many a lonely night. It's good to see you, too, he said, breathing as hard. As eager.

She unhooked her arms from around his neck and took a step back to look at him.

You're shaking, she said.

Hadn't stopped since I saw you.

What were you afraid of?

That you might not want to see me. That you wouldn't be here. I mean, that you would but you wouldn't. He tried to read her thoughts in her eyes, but saw nothing he could know.

I'm here, she said, taking another step back and narrowing her eyes. But are you?

I haven't ever really left, he said, knowing he was wide the mark.

Jo Shelby Ferguson! she said in a voice loud enough to echo off land flat as the Delta. For six years I didn't see you, then saw you a handful of hours and you were off to Mexico like some hair-brained idiot.

You read the same letters. You said you'd have gone, too if you thought you had family somewhere else in the world.

I did say that, but—

And I came back, he said.

Her face was one of exasperation; one he didn't know how to solve. He looked down, kicked at a clod of disked field with his boot toe, as if breaking it down might reveal a clue.

She tried to help. Jo Shelby, before you left, the few hours we were together, I did not really know who you were. I wanted to, kept asking myself, who is this person? What did prison do to him? What sort of man did it make of him? Did he change? Is he worse? Better? Is he all right? Who is he?

Guess I was asking those same questions. That's why I had to go.

Well! Did you get any answers?

Her eyes were bearing down on him, her words whittling on him, like he was something that needed paring down to size. I can think better sittin down, he said. Why don't we sit down?

You used to say you could think better standing up.

He remembered the fights when they were growing up, when she was the one wanting to sit and he was the one wanting to stand. I'm not used to standing and thinking this long, he said.

This long? she said, her voice louder, her eyes bristling. Six months. One letter. I gave you my phone number. No calls. Nothing. I had no idea what happened to you. Then all of a sudden you're back and I find you out here, practically in my own backyard, and you weren't sure I wanted to see *you*. How do you think *I* felt.

Guess we just mis-guessed each other, he said and looked down at his feet.

She grabbed him by the shoulders and shook him and he looked up. But thank God you are here, she said, her voice calmer as she reached up and touched his face with her hand. You've lost weight. Then she leaned in close and examined his mouth. And your front teeth are gone. Your mouth looks terrible. How did that happen?

It's a long story, he said. It's why I didn't write but one letter.

Well, it'd better be a good one, a mockery in her voice.

He picked up his hat, dusted it against his leg and put it back on. Now can we sit down?

They sat on the ground beside the small cemetery, the horses standing nearby, the night developing slowly around them, light enough still to see each other's faces. She sat immobile, her eyes fixed upon his, a look of wonderment in them as he told her the story of his long search, its many twists and turns before he found Senora Moncada, the last remnant of his family. She asked about his return trip, the places he stopped along the way, where he slept, ate, why it took him so long getting back. One by one he answered her questions. He made broad strokes, gave no details. He avoided any mention of Christmas in Mexico City, who he'd stayed with and how long. She listened with that certain regard in her eyes, one that looks through the story and senses there is more than is being told. When he was through it was dark. In the distance car wheels whined across a macadam. Nearby insects whirred electrical sounds.

Silence fell and stretched.

They sat looking at each other, at shapes. He knew where they needed to go next. She probably did, too. But neither knew how to get there. That was the silence.

They let it grow until it became too heavy for him and he finally decided to try, even if he stumbled. You know why I didn't call or come by.

Jo Shelby, I said all I could about that before you left. I can only apologize for my daddy so much. There just wasn't much he could do.

It wasn't what he did, he said. It was what he didn't do. What he didn't say to the sheriff. Mr Sheriff, y'all investigate this thing a little longer. Mr Sheriff, I really think you got the wrong feller here. He didn't lift a finger to write the gov'ner for an early parole. Didn't come see me when I was in. Wouldn't let you come see me. Didn't do diddly. He was feeling the anger rise in his voice and knew he needed to stop. He'd already stumbled.

Do you hate him? she said.

No. I don't hate him. I don't hate anybody.

But you don't like him.

I don't have a feeling about him. He's not the reason I got put in prison. I was at the wrong place at the wrong time. He just didn't help when I got in and you and I both know why.

She reached over for his hand and held it. He and mama were just being protective of me, she said softly. But they don't run my life anymore.

They did once, he said. Wouldn't let you drive five miles to see me. You could've even ridden a horse to the property line and waved at me in the fields.

That was a long time ago.

Yesterday.

She let go his hand. Maybe to you, she said. Seems like a long time to me. It's why I don't know you. Then you got out and took off like a crazed maniac. I didn't know if you were dead or alive until I got your letter. That was months ago, not yesterday. I thought I'd hear something else, at least a phone call. But nothing. I had to get on with my life.

What's that supposed to mean? They were close. The dark was getting darker. He could only see her shape.

You're not the only one in this world who's got a long story, Jo Shelby Ferguson.

You listened to mine, he said.

She bowed her head and looked down a while. He couldn't see them when she raised up, but he could hear the tears in her voice. When you think of prisons, she said, you think of walls and barbed wire and guards and guns. You don't think of flat wide open space walled in by ideas centuries old. You don't think of a way of life that hasn't changed in hundreds of years, and never will. You don't think of doing the same thing over and over, day in and day out. Of spending money that's not there, drinking and dancing and partying till the sun rises. Going to the same places, seeing the same people, listening to the same stories. While you were serving time in one prison, I was growing up in another one next door. In a strange and twisted way, I thought you were blessed, that you missed six years of all that. I wish I had. I don't intend to spend the rest of my life in this prison, she gestured, pointing toward the ground.

The chill he felt came not from the night air. All was quiet about them, the horses mute but for their breathing. When he spoke his voice seemed lost. So where will you spend it? Before I left, you were going to be a teacher in Atlanta. You still goin?

She didn't answer him.

If you don't spend it here, he said, mimicking her gesture toward the ground, you goin to Atlanta?

I don't want to talk about that right now. You're back and I'm glad to see you. Let's do something else. Something we used to enjoy. Let's ride.

As they stood he drew her close, placed a finger beneath her chin and guided it upward toward his face, found her lips with his and felt, once more, that first and last kiss on earth he remembered before he left and in that brief moment it seemed nothing had changed. Though everything had, he feared.

By the way, she said, as they were mounting their horses. Speaking of letters, there's one at the house for you from Mexico. We saved it, just in case.

He froze in the saddle. If it was from Carmen, that might explain a thing or two. If it was from Carmen and Athen read it, that might explain more than a thing or two. Then again, Athen would never read another's mail. Still the thought nagged at him, who the letter was from and the news it might bring.

She pulled on her reins to lead the way and he stopped her.

Athen, I saw lights on in my old house. Mr Bo said your daddy had a new foreman.

He does. Mr Ligon and his family. But he can't hold a candle to your daddy, his wife to your mama either. Daddy and Mama have missed them. We all have. The place just hasn't been the same.

Same. The word resonated, the sound of it suddenly disquieting, a reminder of all that wasn't, and never would be.

Side by side they rode, their horses matching stride for stride beneath the cloudless star-sprinkled sky, where the Lord had punched pinholes so He could look down, his mother had told him. He let Athen move ahead, observed her poised erectness in the saddle, her dark hair leveling out behind her, the grace she brought to the horse, to the night. To him.

They slowed the horses on the field road they'd been on a while, then turned south where it T-boned with another. He galloped past her and led the way. At the southern edge of the plantation where it abutted the fenceless boundary of the penitentiary he stopped. He'd always wondered why Parchman didn't have fences, then once inside understood. There was nowhere for a man to run in seventeen thousand acres of flat open space, where a rifle site could nail him and drop him in his tracks with a single shot.

He leaned forward in the saddle and looked. At the flush expanse of darkness. At the prison towers beyond it, lit up like giant fibrous insects from an outer space movie. He removed his hat and wiped his brow and sat, continued looking, his eyes adjusting better to the dark now that he was stationary. Even in the night he could see them, their darker texture running up against the rim of the lighter sky, the fields he'd worked as a prisoner and recalled having to look across that unmarked perimeter at ones he'd worked as many years. His parents had sent him into the fields when he was twelve years old and he went thereafter each summer to hoe and each fall to pick and rode horses with his father in the winter months. He'd worked both sides of that invisible line and for a moment contemplated life in the mansion behind him. Its set routines. Its known qualities. What Athen had called it and the land it ruled as he swung his eyes back on the prison lights.

She came loping to a halt beside him. Did you really want to stop here? she said.

Yep.

The horses were breathing hard from the ride and nothing else could be heard except the sporadic whir and murmur of night creatures in the fields.

I'd think you'd never want to see that place again, she said.

I need to see it. Don't need to ever forget it.

He pulled on the bridle reins and turned his horse. She did likewise with the palomino. Side by side they held their horses still. Stiller in their saddles they sat as they watched the sight unfold against the deep purple sky, a full orange moon booming upward out of the east, leaving the land and trees and anything else that touched the sky, like a bright balloon turned loose by a hidden god. He reached for her hand and she reached back and they sat speechless atop the horses and together beheld the spectacle.

I think that's the most beautiful moon I've ever seen, she said.

Mighty hard to beat, he said then told her about one he'd seen on the river barge on his way to Mexico that might come close. This would be a good time to ask about Atlanta he thought then thought again, another plan blooming in his brain, beating the moon to its ascendancy. Wear her down first.

Like you said, let's ride, he said and popped his heels into Midnight's flanks.

Beneath the jeweled bowl of sky, across the moon-chalked level land they rode, over crop roads and fields and trails they had ridden before, the memorized geography of their youth, years that seemed magically erased by it all, by the smells of the rich broken earth and the cool breeze, by the anonymous night. At one point he looked at her and she looked back at him, mirror images of beat-me-if-you-can and the race was on.

They rode as they'd never ridden before, as if life and death depended on who won. He thought he'd left her in the dust then heard the percussions coming up behind and glimpsed her sliding into view, her body flat against her horse's neck, her hair streaming behind her, gliding past him like the figurehead of a ship passing in the dark. Over the crop roads they rode. He'd gain some then slip, gain then slip, the story of his life he thought as he urged Midnight on. He was the one who'd started it and it looked as though she'd be the one to end it. Far ahead of him she slowed, wheeled her horse and trotted back to join him, her smile a bright lasso thrown from the dark.

You satisfied now Mr Jo Shelby Ferguson? She sat straight in the saddle, unruffled, her face awash in the moonlight. She wasn't even breathing hard.

Guess you won that one, he said.

Don't I always?

Not always. I have a time or two.

A time or two.

He thought of his plan and there she sat looking fresh as the sky. So, where is it, this place you plan to spend your life? he said, no longer able to hold back.

My, my. Where'd that come from?

It came from back yonder at the cemetery, he said, nodding in that direction, when you wouldn't tell me if you were goin to Atlanta or not. I'm just wantin to finish it off.

There's nothing to finish off, that edge in her voice again. I wish you'd just let it go.

Best way for me to let it go is for you to tell me.

All right, she said. I finish my degree this May. I've been offered a job teaching in Atlanta, starting this September.

Offered. Didn't say you were takin it.

Jo Shelby, that's in September, six months away. A lot can happen in six months.

I know how long six months is, what all can happen.

Even if I did, I could come home on weekends.

Sounds like you're goin.

Jo Shelby, hush up. I'm not going to listen to this. We need to get on back. Mama and Daddy'll start worrying about me.

They oughtta be worrying, all right, he was thinking, feeling his anger rise. He glanced in the direction of the big house and the buildings surrounding it, their dark silhouette that of a small village cut and pasted against the sky. He wondered if he should tell her now what was brewing, the history that was about to unravel around her if his great-great-great granddaddy's name was not on a deed in the county courthouse, then decided not. She might sure as hell go to Atlanta, sooner than later.

All right, he said, flicking the reins of his horse, falling into a slow trot and pulling even with her. They pushed the horses into a lope toward the lights of the compound and rode in silence, the moon high in the sky, bright as a spotlight, casting a silky phosphorescence across the land.

They stopped at the barn. This is as far as I need to go, he said.

Why don't you get down and come in, at least say hello to mama and daddy. Sissy's there. She'll want to see you.

He sat in the saddle and thought. He would like to see Sissy. Her name was Cassie Mae. Everyone else called her Cassie but Sissy was all he could manage as a child, the way it came out when he tried to wrap his small mouth around the long name. And there was the letter from Mexico. He did need to get that. He pulled out his pocket watch, angled it under the thin light of a single bulb hanging over the loft bay. It was almost seven. All right, he said. But not for long. I'm supposed to eat supper with Mr Bo and Miss Floy at seven.

They left the horses tied to a post beside the barn. He followed her up the path from the barn to the house, across the patio and through the back door into the kitchen where Sissy was tending the stove.

Lawd, lawd, Mr Jo Shelby, she cried out. If you aint a sight to behold. She put her fleshly arms around him; near smothering his face in her breasts then released him. We thought you'd done gone for good. My, my, if this aint some surprise.

Athen led him down a polished hallway and into the elegant and well-to-do world he'd only guessed about in his thoughts and dreams. He followed her past a spiral staircase, beneath a crystal chandelier and in to the den; a large windowless room with a huge stone fireplace, heavy cushioned leather chairs and dark carved furniture, plush carpet. A couple of family portraits in gilt frames hung on one wall. The heads of animals killed as sport decorated another. He inhaled the thick air, the enclosed odor of spent cigars and furniture polish and winter ashes, of pride and order and immodest hopes. A room like the warden's office at the penitentiary, one that said power. One that said don't trespass but he'd already crossed that line.

Look who's finally back, Athen said.

Mr Pat was reading a newspaper and Miss Pat flipping through a magazine. Mr Pat rose slowly from his chair, his large frame emerging from it as if with great effort, and shook Jo Shelby's hand limply. His black hair was combed back straight and slick as ever, his deep-set eyes as hooded, as brooding. Glad to see you made it back, boy, he said, the tone of his voice weak as the handshake.

Miss Pat's plucked-to-a-thread eyebrows flew up like wings, her painted mouth a perfect 0, as round as the perfectly painted face, all of it looking that rehearsed. We had no idea what happened to you, she said, her caught-off-guard voice struggling to sound friendly, her mouth quivering between a smile and a frown. Her mouth twitching like it too, like something caught in a trap. A gambling man of no renown would play the odds on the frown, that that's how the face would turn up when her emotions quit rolling and came to a stop. Snake eyes. She remained seated and extended a dainty bejeweled hand he held briefly, slightly bowing, bestowing to her that ingrained deference he'd learned as a child.

He recalled the warm send-off six months before, compared it with the sudden chill and put it all together. He was a problem they thought had gone away and here it was back on their doorstep.

Without waiting to be told, Sissy brought him a tall glass of iced water from the kitchen, then departed, knowing her place in the hierarchy of the house.

He's only got a minute, Athen said. He's got to be back at Bo and Floy's for supper.

Bo and Floy's? Miss Pat said.

That's where I'm stayin, Jo Shelby said. For right now, anyhow.

You could stay in the garage apartment, Miss Pat said. It hasn't changed since the night you stayed before you left

I'm much obliged, he said. They got one, too.

Seconds went by and nothing was said. Mr Pat sat back down in his chair. Miss Pat opened the magazine she had closed but she wasn't turning the pages.

I understand I got a letter here, Jo Shelby said, sensing an opportunity might slip away.

He said it looking at no one in particular, but Miss Pat responded. Why yes, I believe you do. Cassie, she called out.

Sissy came shuffling again from the kitchen into the den.

Mr Jo Shelby's got a letter, Miss Pat said. It's on the mantel in the living room. Would you get it please?

Yessum, Sissy said and departed, her wide body moving the air in the big room as she crossed it then returned as quickly, handing the letter to Miss Pat who, in turn, handed it to Jo Shelby. Sissy had walked right past him, could have easily handed it to him herself. But that was the Delta, the complex transference evoking the reason the sheriff had to have a planter's permission to come on his property. The reason Athen couldn't visit him in prison without her father's accompaniment. The reason coloreds and whites drank from separate fountains and ate in separate restaurants and sat in different places. The sum total reason the social ladder in the Delta was bottom heavy on the lower rungs and light at the top. That it would fall if the lower rungs decided they wanted to be on top.

He held the envelope beneath a lamp shade nearby, studied the handwriting, the Republica del Mexico stamp and postage mark that said Monterrey, then the return address:

Senor Jose Ramon Garcia
206 Esteban
Monterrey, Mexico

Who's it from? Athen said.

He continued gazing at the envelope. Ramon, my friend I was telling you about.

The one who got you out of prison? she said.

Prison? Mr Pat said. Were you in prison again?

He didn't do anything wrong, Daddy, Athen said. I'll tell you about it later. It was a misunderstanding.

But to answer her question, Jo Shelby said, raising his eyes from the envelope and holding them steady on Mr Pat. He *was* the *one* who helped get me out of prison.

Mr Pat's face went slack, the red showing first in his cheeks then spreading upward across his forehead. Miss Pat began flipping the pages in her magazine. Sissy retreated quickly into the kitchen.

Athen stood in momentary disbelief, her eyes alternating between her father and Jo Shelby. Then she pointed at the letter. Aren't you going to open it and read it?

Unsure of the letter's contents, the news it might convey, he thought a minute. Never burn your bridges behind you, his daddy always said. He continued holding the letter in his hand, as though weighing it in judgment. Think I'll wait a while, he said. I need to be moseying along.

He bid farewell to Mr and Miss Pat, who raised limp hands into the air. Out of politeness Miss Pat said, you come back to see us. He hugged Sissy again on his way out the kitchen door. In the darkness, with only the porch lights from the back of the house to guide them, he followed Athen back down the same path to the barn, the same path that gave him a clear view of his old home, those memories.

When will I see you again? Athen said.

I believe tomorrow's Sunday. You going to church?

I'd planned to.

He leaned over and kissed her, mounted Midnight and tipped his hat. See you in church then, he said, then turned the horse and headed back across the fields, the light of the moon guiding the way.

The Stevens weren't upset he was late. Miss Floy said it just gave her more time to get everything on the table. Everything on the table was country-fried steak and gravy, biscuits made from scratch, mustard greens, cornbread, black-eyed peas, speckled butter beans and mashed potatoes. Miss Floy must have known how long it had been since he'd had home-cooked food. After apple pie and ice cream he told them goodnight, thanked them for making him feel at home.

He entered the apartment and saw the covers were turned back, clean white sheets on the bed, clean underwear folded neatly atop them along with a pair of pajamas that weren't his. His corduroy pants and shirt hung from a hanger on a window ledge, neatly ironed. He'd bought them in Mexico City when he bought the hat and thought it a small wonder Miss Floy could make them look new after all they'd been through.

The ride, tacked onto the long day, had made him tired and he decided to go straight to bed and wash up in the morning, be fresh for church. He removed his clothes and laid them carefully over the back of a chair, slipped into the checkered flannel pajamas. They were a little loose, but they'd do. He climbed under the sheets and retrieved the letter from the nightstand where he laid it. He checked the postage mark before opening it. 14 Febrero, 1955. Almost a month to get here, he thought, then remembered that was what the hotel clerk in Cuernavaca had said when he gave him the letter to mail to Athen. He held the envelope up to the light, made an even tear down one side and removed three folded pages.

He was thankful it was in English, his Spanish having faded some during his return. Use it or lose it his father had once remarked humorously, about something far removed from the task at hand. He hoped he never lost his Spanish. He might need it again some day. He held the first page under the lamp and began reading.

14 February 1955

Estimado Señor Jo Shelby,

Greetings from Monterrey. Señora Garcia and I send to you our best wishes and hope you arrived to your destination safely. Please let us know because we worry about you, the señora especially. She thinks you are a very kind and good person, but much too reckless. She thinks that of me as well, so not to worry.

We enjoyed very much the time you spent with us, particularly all the nice things you said about Carmen. She was much impressed with you. The señora thinks more than impressed. I do not know. I am not trying to, as they say, play the cupid. But enough of our women.

I have been out of the prison now almost four months.

Some things have happened since you left. A few days after your departure, the guard who helped arrange our exit was killed. You will never guess. Carlos (the same who tried to kill you) knifed him at the gate when he refused to let him see his mother and sister. Of course, Carlos was executed almost immediately. There are no courts, no procedures in prison for something like this. I learned of this unfortunate event from one of my former students who keeps me informed.

Also, Señor Jo Shelby, I did write to the gun collector in Cuernavaca, the address you gave to me. He wrote back to me and said, as you told me, that he would hold the gun for six months then sell it back to you for one hundred American dollars, but would not hold it longer than six months, that he already had interested buyers. I do not believe he does, but that is what he said. He will let me buy the gun for you and return it to you.

We, of course, do not have one hundred dollars. Carmen wants to go to him and buy it for you.

Well, I'll be a son of a gun, he said, lowering the letter to his lap. She's gonna take care of my gun after all. He brought the letter back into his vision and began reading again.

She told me of her effort to get you to pawn it in Mexico City where she could keep a closer watch on it, but she said you were more stubborn than a burro. I laughed. She and her mother would make two burros look like the Ned in the first reader, or something like that, as you were so fond of saying. Regardless, you have Carmen's address. It is best, I think, you communicate with her about the gun.

She is in a much better position than I to help you.

The hell he's not playing the cupid, he whispered to himself.

Now something about myself and my situation.

We do not know if our mail is being opened and inspected. It has been in the past. But I do not think they would be suspicious about a letter from your country.

He reached over and picked up the envelope where he'd left it on the bed beside him, held it up against the lamplight again. Nothing seemed unusual about it, no extra tears, indications it might have been pried open and resealed. He continued reading.

I am keeping a very low profile. That is best for now.
But there are plans being made, good plans. I was happy to hear about your plans to run for political office in Mississippi.

He glanced away. I'm not running for any office, he said to himself, then looked back at the page.

It is very commendable that you run. You will make a great governor of your state.

If that doesn't beat all. It's code. The old codger's gonna run for governor of his own state, Nuevo Leon. He laid the letter down again and reflected on all he knew of the man, of his history and his family's history, people trying to help their own, trying to do right in a country where right had such little history. He didn't know how a man could go from being a prisoner to being a governor without all the in-between, but he guessed they just did things different in some countries, that there wasn't any in-between, just a lot of guts and luck. Or that being a prisoner in Mexico made you better qualified. Or it made you famous. He thought about himself and his plans and decided he and Ramon were both brothers of revolution, destined to have known one another, destined to do the unthinkable.

I will look forward to hearing from you about your campaign. That is all for now, my dear amigo. Please write to us. Be safe.
God go with you.
Your amigo,
Jose Ramon Garcia

He turned out the light and said his prayers, thanking the good Lord for where he was and what he had and watched the moon through the window on its way to the top of the sky as he thought about church tomorrow and how it would feel. Then of Athen going back to school and how that would feel. Then he thought no more as the dark and the ticking of the clock claimed him.

He stood and waited for her in the drive by the red Thunderbird he'd helped load. Boxes of shoes and toiletries. Assorted clothes. Nice dresses she was going to wear somewhere, with somebody. A woman didn't dress up like that and go by herself. She'd asked him to come with her. He needed to go to college and get a degree and could enroll for summer semester, she said. He could look for a job there and she would find a place for him to stay, she said. She said he needed this and he could do that and why didn't he do such-and-such. She said it all with eyes of compelling sincerity, a mother's urgency in her voice, as if this was his last chance to make something of himself and there was nothing in all she said that sounded like it had anything to do with land or farming.

He was tempted, had already tempted himself before she started in, thought of all the arguments for and against, run them up and down that over-worked adding machine in his head, pulled the handle and the answer that clicked into place was not the one he wanted to see. He'd shift the options around and run them again and the answer was still the same. Even if he started to college now, she'd be four years ahead of him. There was already the time separating them plus his four years plus time studying, time driving back and forth from somewhere, Atlanta probably, trying to see each other. Time he didn't have because he was running in the biggest catch-up race of all time.

He'd tried to think about it in church, how to present to her the plan he'd concocted. But the small sanctuary was too full of distractions, of his life. The same pew. Same smells. Except for the preacher, a student pastor from Delta State, the same people. Same little old purpled-hair lady clanking out the same songs on the same out-of-tune piano. Same can be a comfort, but it can also be an agony, the memories that press against you. He'd tried to think, but all he could do was feel.

By the time Athen finally came bounding through the patio door, Mr and Miss Pat had come out and were standing there, watching. Overseeing.

She hugged him, told him she'd see him next weekend, all of it right there in front of them. They, by damn, might not own her after all, he thought as he watched her pull away in the sleek car, down the long drive, through the brick gate and out of his life, it seemed, the world around him suddenly that empty.

II

The Delta at dawn. There was nothing like it anywhere. First flush of light on a horizon straight as if God had laid down a ruler and drawn it. First shafts shooting upward from behind it like a bomb going off on the other side of the world, firing the clouds pink and yellow and orange until the whole eastern sky seemed one huge bonfire. Then that first cusp of brilliant light, old as time, bright as a welder's arc bulging into the fading dark, its rays streaking across the flatness and you seeing them before anybody else in the world, before they struck beaches or ocean waves or touched the tops of the great mountains because there was nothing in between to stop them as they raced that straight and true across the earth, that pure and unobstructed and undefiled.

He stood at the window of the small apartment and watched, remembering something he'd heard on the tanker crossing the Gulf on his way to Mexico. Red sky at morning, sailor take warning. It meant bad weather was coming. He wished that was all it meant. Bad weather. You could ride out a storm thrown at you from the heavens. It was the ones blowing up from within that way laid you, twisted heart and soul beyond recognition, beyond anything you could unravel by yourself.

He bathed and dressed, brushed his teeth, recalling what Athen had said about them. It *was* an awful gap, made him look like one of Spanky's gang in the movies. He stood a while longer assessing himself in the mirror, at how old his face had grown in such short time. He leaned in closer for a better look. Sure enough, they were there. Wrinkles. Tiny thread-like lines spreading from the corners of his eyes. Thin blond welts beneath the lower lids, as if a miniature whip might have lashed him there, leaving fine wisps of scars. The skin around the sockets looked darker, as though seared, and he thought of Senora Garcia's eyes, how all the pain in her life seemed funneled to them, as though it had wandered through her body and finally settled around her eyes, badges for the world to see, her witness to endurance, that that's what it looked like, endurance, the color of something that had been fired and blasted and scorched and was still standing. Gun metal came to mind.

He leaned away from the mirror and combed his hair, patted an errant strand into place, adjusted the collar of his shirt. He needed to look like a respectable citizen and not some roustabout redneck with a half-cocked hair-brained idea.

Mr Bo had told him he could have the day off to run errands and stock his apartment. He would do all that when he got back, he told Mr Bo. First he needed to go to Indianola on business. Mr Bo had that look he understood, as one looks when he knows a shared secret then drove him to the highway where he could hitch a ride.

It was not yet six o'clock and traffic almost non-existent. In minutes that seemed hours he stood by the side of the road, his thumb out. Before long a teenager in a red two-door hard top Chevy with fenderskirts, spinner hubcaps and dual antennae on the rear fins picked him up. He asked the kid what he was doing up so early and the kid, who looked to be not a day over fourteen, told him he hadn't gone to bed, that he'd been to a party at Ole Miss.

They party on Sunday up there? Jo Shelby said, recalling all the nice dresses and shoes he'd help Athen pack.

They don't never stop.

You in school there?

Naw. I'm just a junior in high school.

You're mama and daddy not worried about you?

Aint got none. Both of em dead, killed in a car crash a few years back. Live with my grandmama.

He wished he hadn't asked. There was enough pain in his life without scratching up more. He wondered about all the orphaned children in the world and how they made it and whispered a quiet prayer of thanks to the Lord that he'd had his mama and daddy long enough to bring him up right. He looked at the boy who had a crew cut and pimples the size and color of raspberries on his face. Your grandmama don't care? he said.

Naw. She don't know. Goes to bed late and sleeps late. By time I git there and fix my breakfast she'll just think I'm gittin ready for school.

The boy let him off in Drew and he walked down the highway toward the end of the town. An older man picked him up and dropped him off at Doddsville and by seven thirty he'd made it to Indianola and the courthouse, where he'd have to wait another thirty minutes for the doors to open.

He stood at the wide doors with a group of colored folk also waiting to get in. Their clothing was old and soiled and tattered, a patchwork of unmatched pieces that hung from them like something carelessly thrown on stick scarecrows. They mumbled a shy low greeting to him. He tipped his hat and returned the diffident salutation, assayed what reason they could have for wanting in a courthouse, what they might own that would give them reason. Or like him, might not own. He thought of how they came to be, how everyone came to be, lives drawn from one big hat of fate, some lucky but some not ... most not. He thought the group before him sure as hell got a bad draw and how God ought to let them step up to the hat and draw again. He thought of the campesinos in Mexico, of their struggle for a scrap of earth to claim as their own and wondered why there weren't *ejidos* in America, plots of land taken from the rich by the government and given to the poor, why somebody at the state capitol in Jackson or the big one in Washington hadn't stood up and proclaimed it. His daddy called it laying down the law but now, observing the group again, their threadbare and raveled decrepit state, he thought it should be called standing up the law. The law was sure enough lying down. It was sleeping.

At eight o'clock sharp a nicely dressed lady opened the double doors. Jo Shelby held one for the Negroes and motioned for them to progress ahead of him, figuring that was the least he could do at the house of law for a law that did nothing for those who had nothing. They bowed as they thanked him, regarded him with looks of shocked gratitude, expressions that carried, too, a hint of suspicion, of fear. He would recall the incident long after its occurrence, would recall their ruined state, their surprised apprehensive faces stooping to him, wondering whether the fear he detected in their eyes was for him or them, or that whole world of greed and bondage. And, too, what business they might have had that day, wishing he had asked.

He'd been with his father before and knew where to go. The Chancery Clerk's office was on the first floor, a large room that reminded him of the Regristro in Cuernavaca, Mexico. He walked up to the long counter, removed his hat and asked the lady who'd opened the door for the clerk. She said the clerk hadn't made it in but that she was Mrs. Shaw, an assistant, and could she help him.

I'm looking for a land deed.

What kind of deed? Warranty deed, quit deed? There are different types.

Though he'd gone with his father, his father always made him sit on one of the benches outside, so he was never privy to the discussions inside, never got wind of the kind of deed. A deed was a deed. But it was all about land so he conjured up a guess, trying to look and sound as if he knew what he was talking about.

I guess just a regular one. It'd be old. Don't know exactly what it's called.

You must mean a warranty deed. How old is it? she said. One courthouse burned and the county seat moved a couple of times before coming to Indianola, except it wasn't called Indianola then but Indian Bayou. That was in 1882. A lot has happened to the county records.

He felt he was back in Mexico and its tangled web of lost and destroyed and misplaced records. He guessed it was like that the world over, so much history missing because nobody cared enough to pack it up and see that it got from place to place as the center of power moved. If his family could save letters a hundred years old, it would seem a government could save something as important as a deed. But his heart sank when he heard her say the date.

So you don't have anything before 1882?

Oh, yessir. We have them back to 1871, when the county seat moved to Johnsonville.

That's about right, he said, his heart pumping again. I'm looking for one that would have changed hands in 1875, somewhere round about then.

That *is* a long way back. May I ask the reason?

Yessum, he said then told her the short version of the story, how his great-great- grandfather Foster Ferguson lost the plantation in 1875 on a gambling bet to a Yankee named Marshall but that the property may not have been Foster's to lose, much less deed to another and that that was why he was there, to get to the bottom of it, if there was one.

My, my, she said. That is some story.

About that time, a tall slender man entered the room through a door at the rear. He looked to be in his seventies and wore a blue coat and maroon tie and had a large nose the color of the tie. He walked with a limping swagger favoring his left leg and Jo Shelby saw his left shoe had an elevated sole.

Mister ... I don't believe I got your name, the lady said.

I never said it. It's Ferguson. Jo Shelby Ferguson. He wanted to keep talking to the woman. She seemed genuinely interested and caring. She wanted to help him. But the situation shaping up was dimming that prospect.

Good morning, Lucille, the man said with a deep strong voice that contradicted his aging beanpole appearance as he stepped up to the counter beside the woman.

Mr Doom, this is Mr Jo Shelby—

Ferguson, Jo Shelby said, helping the woman out as she drummed a nervous finger on the counter trying to tap in his last name. Jo Shelby Ferguson. Mighty pleased to meet you, and he extended a hand across the counter.

Yessir, the man said again, smiling as he reached across to accept the handshake. I'm Roy Doom, chancery clerk. Chancery clerk for forty-three years. Know nearly everybody in this county but don't reckon I know you.

Now, what can I do for you Mr Jo Shelby Ferguson? Once I say it, I don't ever forget a person's name.

Jo Shelby had never heard the man's name. His father just always called him the clerk. The clerk this, clerk that, as though he didn't need another name. If he'd been there nearly half a century, he sure to God was the clerk and didn't need another name. Then the gears of arithmetic began turning in his head and the man's name began weighing on him, like a pronouncement.

Mr Doom, Mr Ferguson wants to check on an old deed, the woman said.

The man appraised Jo Shelby with speculative eyes. That's good, Lucille. I'll take it from here.

The woman seemed disappointed as she left and returned to a desk in the back of the large room. Not as disappointed as Jo Shelby, looking up into a face turned suddenly serious, as if after some shuffling the clerk had come up with his name after all.

So, you want to check on a deed, Mr Doom said, spreading his arms and planting his hands possessively on the counter, like a challenge, a dare.

Yessir.

And what deed might that be?

Like I told the lady, it goes back to 1875, so the name on it'll be old.

I reckon so. And what name might that be?

Calvin Ferguson. Colonel Calvin T. Ferguson.

I see, the clerk said, cocking his head back into his shoulders, his arms still aspread the counter like a preacher behind a pulpit suddenly smitten with revelation. You don't have you an attorney?

It wasn't a straight out question, but one that slid from the side of his mouth, a feeler question, like a bluff to a man's hand by raising the stakes to see if he means business. Didn't know I needed one, Jo Shelby said, careful to say no more than was necessary.

Don't have to, the clerk said, his face falling into strange lines. But records that old are pretty tricky. We still got some of em, but some we don't. A lot happens over the years, you know.

Jo Shelby looked up at the man, tried to discern what scheme of deception was germinating behind his eyes, the word tricky still resonating. It was the response his father had told him he kept getting. But Jo Shelby knew more than his father knew. He knew the old colonel was alive in 1875.

Yessir, I understand. But I caint afford an attorney. He wasn't lying, he reasoned. He couldn't afford one, not outright. Nothing wrong with slipping a little deception under the deception being laid on him, throwing in a touch of pity along with it.

Tell you what, the clerk said. Give me a little more information and I'll see what I can do for you. What name's the property in now?

The man asked the question as if he already knew the answer, just had an inborn need to go through the formality.

Mr Jack Patrick.

Jack Hurley Patrick, Jr.?

Yessir. His daddy owned it before him and before that it belonged to a man named Marshall from up north and before that to my great-great-great granddaddy, the name I just told you, Calvin Ferguson. Cept he went to Mexico and while he was away the place burned and my great-great granddaddy, Foster Ferguson, lost the property in a gambling match, cept it wasn't his to lose and that's what I'm aimin to trace and find out. He wanted to slap himself for saying more than he meant, but the words were gone, echoing through the large lighted chamber of leather-back volumes the size of concrete slabs, arousing the attention of everyone within earshot who stopped whatever they were doing and snapped their attention on him. He might as well have blown a bugle that said charge, fired a cannon to announce his attack.

Sounds like you got this down pretty good, Mr Doom said, a flash of amazement in his eyes. I don't think you'll need an attorney after all. Let me see what I can do. Come back in a few days.

Y'all not open on Saturdays, are you?

Nope. Closed tight as a jail, he said with a cunning smile.

Don't know when I can get back. But I'll be back.

He exited the same doors he'd entered, made his way through a small gathering of loafers on the porch hunched over in conversation in old captains' chairs he guessed the county provided for that purpose. To keep them off the marble-polished floors and out of the marble-polished halls that told you how small you were when you stepped through the wide double doors and into the smell of power, because nothing else had an odor like that. That claimed you with its history.

He was kicking himself on his way to the highway for saying more than he meant to say. But Mr Roy Doom, clerk of forty-three years, should be doing as much to himself. For letting one Jo Shelby Ferguson know he was afraid of an attorney.

He sure doesn't want any lawyer sniffin 'round in those records, Jo Shelby said. Upon leaving the clerk's office, he'd made a beeline to Mr Darden's.

Sounds like it, Mr Darden said from behind piles of paper that seemed to have made their way from the floor to his desk. And he sure as hell doesn't want to deal with me.

Afraid I told him more than I meant to, though, Jo Shelby said.

What'd you tell him?

He told him how, after dropping Jack Hurley Patrick's name, he blabbed the history of the place and how the clerk's eyes widened and rolled back in their sockets. But I didn't say the old Colonel was still alive, he said. I don't think I told him that.

Mr Darden swiveled back in his chair and looked at the ceiling. It wouldn't matter if you had, he said. You told him just enough to make him nervous.

Nervous enough to run straight to Mr Pat.

Maybe. Maybe not. Can't tell about county politics. It can change with a sneeze. Besides, Pat's going to find out sooner or later. Is that causing you to have any second thoughts?

No sir. Just didn't want to tip my hand too soon. Besides, I'm not far enough along to have second thoughts. Still working on my first ones.

Well, while you're hammering those down, I've got something to add to the mix.

Yessir.

I've been giving your situation a lot of thought since you left my office the other day, did a little research up here, he said, pointing to his head, and there are a couple of aspects in your favor I didn't think about at the time. It's kind of complicated, so listen up.

Jo Shelby scooted his chair closer to the attorney's desk.

The old Colonel having vacated not only the land but also the country, Foster assumed the land was his and thus the deed. Now the deed wasn't legal and he told Marshall as much, or Marshall was aware of it, but that was at a time when all the legal falderal wasn't worth much anyway, carpetbaggers and scalawags running the South. So Marshall went along with it. Assume, too, the first Patrick when he bought the land from Marshall, knew all this, but time and history were in his favor, his money talked and Marshall walked.

You with me so far?

So far.

The colonel dies in Mexico. He had to die sometime, doesn't really matter when at this point. But he dies and there's no will.

He might've had one. Might've written one in Mexico.

But only God knows that and even if he did it's a needle in some Mexican haystack. But a will would not be enough to revoke title, might even prove more troublesome.

You said if I could come up with one it might stand this thing on its head. I remembered that.

You're right. I did say that. I was talking about a will that hadn't been probated, which still fits with what I'm trying to tell you. The colonel dies and leaves no will or if he did, it's lost somewhere and was never probated. There's a legal term called doctrine of after-acquired title or law of descent and distribution. It goes something like this. If a person dies with no will, the state has one for them and the property is divided in equal shares among the heirs, in this case the children. Therefore, according to Mississippi law, Foster would have acquired only a child's portion, the remaining portions divided equally among the colonel's children.

That'd be the ones in Mexico.

Precisely. How many were there again?

Three. Taylor, Jonathan and Caroline.

So, Mr Darden continued, Foster executed a conveyance but had no right. The colonel dies. Foster inherits an undivided child's part, or one fourth. Now, if he purported to convey that property, the Yankee would have acquired only a child's portion, or one fourth. That's what we mean by doctrine of after-acquired title. You'd have to construct a scenario where the Yankee knew he didn't have clear title, didn't own the land out right and conveyed that to the first Patrick who in turn conveyed it to the second, Jack Hurley, Jr.

That's why my daddy got the runaround every time he went to the courthouse. Why I did this mornin.

Maybe so. But the Fergusons would have had to put Marshall and/or the Patricks on notice.

That's what I aim to do.

I understand. It may be too late for you, but not the descendants in Mexico. They never knew. Therefore, without any knowledge they didn't know of a need to put anyone on notice or stake their claim. In other words, if the folks in Mexico are made aware of all this, it does not favor the Patricks.

They'd just own a fourth, right?

Correct. The other three fourths would pass down by descent and distribution to the surviving heirs on the Mexican side. If you can prove an element of fraud or deceit or that a person knows it isn't their land, you might be able to salvage something. The legal fact there's no statute of limitation on wills in Mississippi makes it even more difficult if there was one dividing the land equally among the siblings. But I think you'd be fishing in a one-fish ocean, for a small fish at that. You have to come up with evidence to negate the current color of title. That's called a cloud on the title. In summary, the statute of limitation is going to run against Foster and his descendants, which means you. But all this other might do something for the folks in Mexico. You'll at least make a showing.

Guess that's the same as putting em on notice?

Absolutely. You'll be making a record. Mary Lou's got the contract up front with her, if and when you're ready to sign and put the gears in motion.

No ifs. Just when. Want to sleep on it a little longer.

* * *

The sun was past mid-sky when he arrived back at the Stevens' and he guessed it was near two in the afternoon. Miss Floy had a tuna sandwich and glass of milk awaiting him and told him Mr Bo would be back mid-afternoon and he could have the truck to run his errands. He took the plate and glass and headed out the door for the apartment but she told him he could eat in the kitchen, that he was like family and not hired help. He thanked her for that, the feeling of gratitude traveling deep inside of him, further than he imagined thanks could go.

It was near four-o'clock when Mr Bo drove up.

Sure you don't need me workin' today, he said. I'm raring to go.

Naw, Mr Bo drawled. It's best if you start fresh in the mornin. Matter of fact, I'm callin it a day, too. Floy wanted me to hoe the vegetable garden out back. Besides, I believe you needed to borrow the truck to run some errands and get your things at the Patrick's. You go ahead and get the rest of your life in order so you can start work tomorrow, hit the ground running.

Yessir. Sure you don't need it.

It'll just sit in the drive. It's not the truck I'm worried about, Mr Bo said, looking back over his shoulder in the direction of the Patrick plantation.

As he drove away he thought about what Mr Bo had said, about getting the rest of his life in order. He'd need more than a pickup and a couple of hours to do that.

It took little time buying his groceries and supplies at the small family-run grocery store in town and by five-o'clock he was at the Patricks'. He stopped the truck beneath the wrought-iron arch and peered up the tree-lined drive. A black Cadillac was parked in front of the proud house, its columns gleaming and white as ever, camellia and jasmine shrubs as immaculate, flowerbeds tidy, everything in its place. Everything except Mr Pat's pickup parked beside the patio. He was supposed to be in the fields.

Jo Shelby waited, idling Mr Bo's truck. He leaned on the steering wheel, tried to gather his thoughts, wondered why there were so many. All he needed was one: I've come to get my things, he would say. He removed his sombrero, dragged a sleeve across his brow, repositioned the hat, then let his foot off the clutch and headed up the drive.

He parked the weather-beaten pickup on the circular drive in front of the house, nose-to-nose the Cadillac, wondering how that looked from the road, what it did to the Gone-with-the-Wind scene. He climbed the red brick steps, knocked his boots against the edge of the polished brick porch. He stood a moment in front of the door, observed his reflection in its oval window. He punched the doorbell button and waited as the chimes ding-donged up and down their same-song scale until the door opened and Sissy appeared.

Lawd, Mr Jo Shelby she cried out. I just seen you t'other day and you still a surprise. She hugged him again. Near smothering him again. Making him recall again those smells and touches of care he'd known growing up.

Sissy, I came to get my trunk. I also left some things in the garage apartment before I left for Mexico, some personal things. But I don't want to bother Mr and Miss Pat.

Sissy rolled her eyes in understanding then leaned in close and whispered. That trunk, it be's in the garage. Them things from the apartment?

Yeah?

I put em in the trunk.

The letters, too?

Miss Pat put those in, figured you were comin pretty soon to git em. I made sure of that, too. Yessiree, chile. Whether you here or not, Sissy gonna look after you. I'll help you with that trunk. She was still whispering, as if hatching a conspiracy.

I don't want to get you in trouble, he said, whispering back, confirming the alliance.

A big smile broke across her face. Honey, you aint gonna git ole Sissy in no trouble. This place'd—she rotated her head comically—fall apart without ole Sissy. But we cain't ever let on we know that, she leaned in and grinned.

She was no longer whispering when she said it and he thought about that as he watched the smile stretch across the large sweat-beaded face, all the way back to her molars. What would they do without Sissy, without all the others, too? The ones in the hundreds of other hot kitchens serving up steaming food, answering every beck and call, cleaning out their johns and scrubbing their floors and ironing their clothes. The ones behind the mules and on the tractors breaking their backs to break the land. The ones that would be in the fields in the fall, toting naked babies under their arms and picking cotton stalks bare so other folks around the world would be clothed. The small gears that made the big gears of their big world turn. What would they do without them? Like Sissy said, nothing. It'd be like one big broken clock. Time standing still.

Sissy, you're an angel sent from heaven. He leaned over and hugged her and she hugged back, a prolonged stout embrace.

I aint no angel, believe you me. But I aim to look after you. She turned and walked back into the house and he reflected on their common histories as he watched her, of the land that bound them together, their families and those before them, that inseparable past to which they were both bonded, and from which they both hoped some day to be free.

He drove around to the side of the big house and backed up to the garage where Sissy was already standing beside an open portal. Mr Pat's truck was still parked beside the patio. Jo Shelby turned off the motor and got out.

The trunk was just inside the door where he'd left it. He grabbed one end and Sissy the other. They had it mid-air to the lip of the tailgate when the screen door slapped shut like a shot and Mr Pat clomped down the steps.

What ch'all doin? he said in a voice louder than was necessary. He was dressed in his neatly pressed khaki planters' clothes, what most planters wore who wanted to look like they were working the land, needed to have that farming look. Like some people wore cowboy boots and cowboy hats and didn't know jack shit about cows.

Just movin this trunk o' his, Sissy said back, as they slid the trunk onto the truck bed.

I don't want to be a bother, Jo Shelby said. Just came to get the trunk and some of my things. I asked Sissy to help me, he said, trying to be protective but Sissy shot him a look she didn't need it.

Not a bother, Mr Pat said, walking towards him. Kinda glad you're here.

Sissy left and returned to the house. Jo Shelby slammed the tailgate shut and began walking toward the driver's side.

Just a minute, Jo Shelby, Mr Pat said. Thought you might like to see the place, what we've done to it since you've been gone. His voice was still friendly, but his eyes had different look.

I really need to get this truck back to—

Naw, now. Come on. Won't take long, he said, putting an arm around his shoulders and guiding him toward his pickup. Your daddy cleared out forty acres on the north side, almost single-handedly. Thought you might like to take a look at it.

Reluctantly, he followed the big man into the cab.

They drove south on the same crop road he and Athen had ridden horses down two nights before, then turned west at the penitentiary line, the pickup bumping and bouncing over the uneven surface. The silence grew heavy inside the cab, like a cloud loading up to drop a storm, Jo Shelby sensing all the while there was another reason for the ride.

Then:

Got a call from Roy Doom, the chancery clerk, this afternoon, Mr Pat said, his voice suddenly serious from his early cheeriness. He said you were down there asking about the deed to the place.

Yessir. He thought about the clerk, how slow he moved on his hobbled foot but how fast his mouth could work.

That true? Mr Pat cast a stern glance at him, eyes that would shine in the dark, then turned them back on the rutted road.

Yessir. He looked over at Mr Pat, at the muscles rippling along his jaw-line, the finer movements over his temple, wishing he could see inside at the cogs and wheels and springs, what they were ratcheting up to so he could think ahead. Instead his thoughts were in reverse, kicking his butt for not having already thought everything out ahead of time.

Guess you got some reason for askin bout a deed. He said it with no more emotion than you'd put into reading an obituary column.

Yessir. His thinking was still stuck in reverse, but if he kept trying, he might come up with something. Or maybe nothing. That might even be better. Just nothing.

And? Mr Pat looked at him again, another warning shot.

I was just askin. It doesn't hurt to ask.

Got no other reason?

Jo Shelby thought again, longer, recalling something his father had told him about Delta politicians, that they only told half-truths. Half to get a step ahead and the other to hold on and use later to keep a step ahead.

No sir, just curious. He hadn't told a lie. That was half-right. But he'd never make it to Delta politician. He couldn't get to the next half.

That's good, Mr Pat said, cause your pa's been down that road before and it's nothin but a dead-end. He said it as the road T-boned at the Stevens' line where they turned and headed north

I wound up in a few of those myself, Jo Shelby said.

Yeah. From what Athen told us, I'd say you have at that.

Don't plan to end up on anymore, either, he said.

Mr Pat was silent, brooding, trying to figure if what he'd just heard was the half he wanted to hear or some other half that kept him guessing. Jo Shelby thought he might make a politician at that.

They rode on.

Nothing was said as they continued north, crossed the macadam highway that split the property and veered back northwest then it got too quiet again. Jo Shelby kept thinking of a way to strike up conversation. He could talk about the weather but there wasn't much to say, except sure is hot for spring isn't it, and the more he thought about that the stupider it sounded, like telling a man a stove would burn him after he touched it. He couldn't talk about the crops. There weren't any yet. He couldn't talk about politics. He didn't even know who the governor was. Religion was out. He didn't remember a thing the preacher had said the day before. Talking about Athen would be like throwing a match in a box of fireworks. Scanning the blank fields and the blank sky something did finally come to him. Where we going now? he said.

Like I said, I want to show you that upper forty your dad cleared out, Mr Pat said, his big shoulders rolling as he spun the steering wheel right so they were headed due north. Then we're gonna find Jake and Josh, he continued. I know they'd like to see you. He turned and glanced at him, one of those sharp looks that's still on you even when its gone, that says I'm keepin my eye on you, boy, gonna watch every move you make. Because that was how everything was beginning to stack up in his thinking. This was going to be war and Mr Pat was going to give him a review of his troops, let him know how tough it was going to be.

They were named for Jacob and Joshua in the Bible his mother had told him Miss Pat told her, but that was about as far as any resemblance to religion got. He'd heard the stories growing up, all the trouble the two boys got into, the drinking, partying, traipsing and cavorting all over the Delta. Both flunked out of Ole Miss, never made it past their sophomore years. Why should they study? They had a daddy who'd given land aplenty to each and a house to boot. Now they were in their mid-thirties, two years apart, almost fifteen years older than Athen, and nothing had changed. Both had beautiful wives and young children. His father once told him you'd think they thought marriage was rental property, the way they moved in and out of it, the wives tolerating the behavior because they liked royalty and all the frills that went with it.

After driving up and down the crop roads of plow-ribbed acreage the size of a small county, looking for two sons nowhere to be found, Mr Pat doubled back from the far perimeter of the place and found both pickups in Jake's driveway.

What the hell you boy's doin'? he hollered after getting out of his truck, motioning Jo Shelby to do likewise. You supposed to be out supervising your teams.

We gittin ready to git this deer outta Josh's truck for Artis to clean, Jake said, looking sheepishly at his father. Josh stood on the other side of the truck bed, his face as concerned. Both were the same size, tall and medium built, handsome faces with their father's strong angular features.

You boys know it's not deer season. Game warden caught you, it'd be a hefty fine.

But the game warden aint comin here, Jake said. We shot it on our place.

How true that was, Jo Shelby thought, neither one of them having fully noticed him yet, their attention too absorbed in an illegal deer and the only person who could turn them in standing ten feet away, who was the law of that land.

I don't give a damn where you shot it, get rid of it. Now!

Jo Shelby had never seen Mr Pat mad before, his face the shade of a watermelon slice, purple veins forking across his forehead, along his temples.

Artis is gonna clean it, Daddy, Jake said. That'll git rid of it.

Artis, hell, Mr Pat said. He's middlebusting. Least he was thirty minutes ago when we were out near the Stevens' line.

Jake and Josh looked at each other waiting for the next to speak, then Jake spoke.

He was. We borrowed him. He's out back settin up to clean this deer.

They had been walking toward the two men but Mr Pat stopped, muttered some profanities under his breath then turned around as though he was going back to his pickup. Jo Shelby wasn't sure what to do, but turned around and followed Mr Pat.

Mr Pat stopped again.

Sorry, Jo Shelby, almost forgot why we came by here. Come on. The boys know you but it's been a while.

Yessir, he said, turned again and followed him back to the two and the pickup, the going back and forth reminding him how he'd followed his own father behind Mr Pat all those years.

You boys leave that damn deer alone for a minute and say hello to Jo Shelby, Mr Pat said. Y'all remember Jo Shelby. He's back, gonna be working down the road with Bo Stevens.

The two men stood looking at Jo Shelby, their attention suddenly drawn to him. Jo Shelby stood looking back. Neither seemed excited to see him. The best defense was a good offense, his daddy had always told him so Jo Shelby stepped forward.

Josh, Jake, how y'all doin? he said, giving each a strong firm handshake, one he wanted them to remember, driving his eyes straight at theirs that were looking down, locking his vision so when they raised up they had to look at him. Not just look at him. Behold him. That was what he wanted them to remember. That they not only saw him and met him but that he made them behold him.

Just wanted y'all to give a friendly Patrick howdy, Mr Pat said. Now get that damn deer to Artis so he can string him up and get back on his tractor.

Jo Shelby watched as they lowered the tailgate and pulled a small deer onto the ground. It looked to be a fawn, not yet a year old, its dark eyes glassy in the sun, like Bambi, Jo Shelby thought. They just don't give a shit. They'd even shoot Bambi. He thought of the picture he'd seen in the lawyer's office and decided there wasn't a magazine deserving of any photo of this. Unless it might be on crime.

What the hell? Mr Pat said, the blood up in his face again. You shoot a deer out of season. Then you shoot a fawn that's a doe, both of those illegal in the State of Mississippi. So you broke three laws. You know what the total fine for all that is?

They shook their heads.

I oughtta turn you in, just to teach you a damn lesson, he shouted, his face almost purple now, the engorged veins taking over the red.

They still said nothing, just bent over and lifted the deer and began toting it toward the back of the house, because they knew he wouldn't. He'd only call the law if it weren't one of his own. Jo Shelby turned slowly and began walking back to the truck, not waiting on Mr Pat. Now was as good a time as any to start walking ahead of him, warm up to wearing that feeling.

It was late in the afternoon, near suppertime, when Mr Pat dropped him back at Mr Bo's pickup.

Don't rush off, stay a spell, Mr Pat said.

Stay a spell, Jo Shelby thought. How long of a spell? He'd ask his mother once when she scolded him, told him to sit in the corner a spell. He asked her if it was a short word or a long word. She told him it was a rest period. Later he'd heard his father use it in the fields, when one worker was relieving another. It was for a short spell. He'd never heard of a long one. Then he went to prison. Thanks just the same, Jo Shelby said as he opened the door to Mr Bo's pickup, got in and slammed it. Need to be mosyin' on. He started the ignition and quickly departed, a realization settling in farther down the road. Mr Pat never did show him the section of land his father had cleared. But he did do something else for him that afternoon. In the army movies he'd seen it was called reconnaissance. Only this time, it was in reverse.

The rest of the week he spent in the fields middlebusting, following the rows, breaking out the stalks. It had been a while since he'd driven a tractor, but it didn't take long relearning the gears, getting the timing and angling on the turn-a-rounds, his rhythm down. Mr Bo started him on an older model John Deere 60, one he'd ridden with his father. Popping Johns they were called because of the way they sounded, going pop, pop, pop, pop constantly, never stopping. They ran on gasoline and had an outside disgage clutch with the crankshaft and gears in the back. All that came back to him. It felt good working again, his body back in the iron saddle, bouncing atop a machine working the earth, open sky ahead, the rich aroma of the land filling his head, the closest a person could get to smelling God his father had once said.

He thought of Athen sixty miles away at college, and again what he would say to her when she returned on the weekend. He wasn't trying to take her daddy's land away from her, which meant hers, too. He was only trying to undo a wrong committed many years ago. He'd worked it all out, what would be fair.

Wednesday a letter arrived from her. It was on his nightstand when he came in from the fields, put there by Miss Floy, he guessed.

He sat on the bed and opened the envelope; soil caked on his hands spattering into it as he pulled out the pages. He turned on the lamp and held a page beneath it and began to read.

Dear Jo Shelby,

I've missed you and wanted to call but didn't want to inconvenience the Stevens. So I decided to write instead.

Classes are dull and the spring weather outside so pretty I find it very difficult studying. I can't wait for this weekend. Get ready because I have some plans for you. First of all, I'm taking you into Clarksdale and help you pick out some clothes. You need a suit and a sport coat and casual slacks and a pair of dress shoes. You're taking me to the Ruleville Club for dinner Saturday night. We'll call it your coming out party.

I enjoyed the horseback ride we had together last Saturday and thought we'd do it again, maybe take a picnic. I haven't ridden much since you've been gone. It brought back a lot of fond, old memories.

Well, so much for now. Hope Mr Bo's not working you too hard. Eat well and sleep well and know I'm thinking of you.

Love,

Athen

He sat a long time holding the pages between his hands, not re-reading them, just looking at them, as though their reality was suspect and required a more thorough, prolonged scrutiny. He'd received letters from her before when he was in prison, but nothing like this, none signed, *Love*. He was near collapse when he sat down, but the energy surging through him could plow another forty acres.

He began reading the letter again then stopped toward the end. The Ruleville Club, he whispered to himself, then again after a long pause. Many times he'd heard his parents speak of it, an establishment halfway between Drew and Ruleville that looked more like a hunting lodge than a restaurant. Where only the cream of the Delta crop went to wine and dine and dance away the nights. Where the state's power broker, Senator Eastland, held court any given evening he wasn't in Washington. Where politicians wheeled and dealed over drinks and cigars deciding the future of everybody that was white, making sure there wasn't one for those less fortunate to have been born black. Where marriages were arranged and unarranged and not a few broken up. Where his father had never taken his mother because he said it was too exclusive and too expensive, that it was not their world, that a man should never be that hungry.

He sat and thought a long while, then on into the night lying in bed, listening to the sounds of the land, its rhythmic whirrs and whispers, its deep throaty croaks and guttural rumblings, its unpretentious flatness, that that was really where he wanted to be, riding side by side with her beneath the moonlight and velvety star-flagged sky. Not at the Ruleville Club.

Friday afternoon came. He was in the fields plowing when he saw the red car streaking toward him, its top down, dust boiling up behind it like smoke spewing from a moving flame. As she got closer he could see her sunglasses and scarf, hair blowing, the composite of it all looking like something off the silverscreen, like someone who knew a camera was following them.

She stopped on the field road not far from him, the cloud of dust overtaking her then vaporizing around her image so she looked like a figment emerging from a mist as she walked toward him, the wind whipping her dress around her thighs and legs, her low-heeled shoes unsteady in the lumpy soil. God did she look beautiful, he thought, as he climbed down from the tractor and walked to greet her.

If you don't look like an angel dropped from heaven, he said. Didn't expect you back this soon.

I was anxious to get home so I cut my afternoon class, she said, then her eyes widened and her mouth fell open. Jo Shelby, your teeth.

Got em back yesterday. Mr Bo let me borrow the truck to go in and get it done. Dr. Dinkler in Drew did a rush job on em.

I'll say. They look wonderful, like they never left.

Some things can look like that. They're just temporaries. He'll put the permanent ones in later, when they come in the mail.

She walked up to him and gave him a hug, her eyes still fascinated with the new teeth.

How'd you find me? he said.

Drove by the Stevens'. Miss Floy said I might find you out this way.

She looked around to make sure they were alone, then reached up and pulled his head down and kissed him. He put his arm around her, held her close, then stepped back.

I'm dirty and sweaty, don't smell good I'm sure, he said, removing his hat and dragging his arm across his forehead.

She took off her sunglasses and looked up at him, her eyes squinting from the sun-glare, her nose scrunched up.

You better put those dark glasses back on. If your face set like that, you would be a sight, look like a frozen sneeze.

She slapped him playfully across the arm and put her sunglasses back on.

He smiled then remembered the concern he'd been churning over all week since his conversation with Mr Pat. You seen your folks?

No, and I won't. At least not until late Sunday.

He held his breath a moment and let it out slowly, trying not to let his relief show.

They've gone to Memphis, she continued. Daddy had a meeting with some cotton buyers and mama went along for the ride, to shop. They decided to spend a couple of nights at the Peabody, go dancing in The Skyway.

Guess that means it's just you and me, he said.

Guess so, she said. Come on down to the house when you finish work and get cleaned up, then pecked him on the cheek walked back to the car.

He watched her drive away in the same fury of dust as she had arrived, knowing she knew his camera eyes were on her.

Surrounded by a grove of cypress and oak and cedar, the lake was an ox-bow, created when the main current of the Big Sunflower took a shorter route, cutting off the shallow crescent-shaped curvature and leaving it abandoned. It had been a favorite picnic spot of his family's, away from the extravagance of the big house and its rowdy and boisterous sounds, a place where windsong and birdsong and the meditative quiet of the dark mirrored water took over a person's mind, leaving the rest of the world behind.

He'd put on clean blue jeans Miss Floy had washed and ironed for him and a clean white shirt, starched at that. He couldn't remember when, in over six years, he'd worn clean clothes more than two days in a row. He'd showered and shaved, put on some cologne he found in the bathroom, Old Spice, probably put there by Miss Floy. She was tending to his every need it seemed as though starved for someone to give it to, her children grownup and flown the coup.

Athens's hair was tied back with a black ribbon and she was wearing blue jeans and a black turtleneck sweater tucked tightly around her waist, her breasts looking fuller than he'd noticed before. They sat on a blanket she'd brought rolled behind her saddle and drank red wine in silver goblets she'd unveiled from gray velvet wraps tied with a fine silver cord and she told him she loved him and he conveyed the same with a nod, his throat too full to speak.

You look sad, she said. What's wrong?

It's not you. Just can't catch up with my grief, much less put it behind me. Me and my mama and daddy and grandmama and granddaddy used to come here a lot. I keep seein things, thinkin I'll get to a point I see em with just my eyes and not deep down.

She put her arm around him, pulled him close. He caught the fragrance of her hair again and decided smell carried more memory than any other sense. Because it was the aroma, too, drifting down from the cedars taking him back. He kissed her again and she kissed him back, a long lingering intermingling of flesh upon flesh, and he tasted the wine again through her lips and wondered what else in this world a man could hope for.

They sat beside each other, sipping their wine, their shoulders touching. The sun was long descending, as though earth and sky had slowed to a crawl. Or maybe his body's inner workings had speeded up causing all else around him to seem in slow motion and he thought of the Mississippi and its unhurried movement and how close he felt to eternity riding it and that love was like a river, too, carrying a body along. Then the sky became a changing sea of color, the clouds floating across it like separate blazing fires slowly burning down as the sun sank lower, finally slipping into the horizon, one gigantic orange disk melting away.

In a ring of lighted candles she'd brought along and planted in the ground around them they sat and ate. Tuna sandwiches and potato chips and dill pickles, a couple of boiled eggs. She kept refilling their cups, as though the bottle had no bottom. Through overhead boughs not yet fully leafed in the early spring they lay on their backs and scanned the cloudless night sky, the stars bright and clear, a half moon beginning its ascent.

A penny for your thoughts, she said, her voice almost a whisper.

He turned his head toward her, the soft features of her face silhouetted in the candleglow. Don't know they're worth a penny, he whispered back.

Then a million dollars.

You aint got a million dollars.

Might someday.

The comment carried the tone of a playful jab but struck him much harder. He squared his eyes back on the sky, her words circulating through his head, then turned and looked at her again.

Athen, how come you love me?

She turned on her side and faced him, her elbow crooked, the side of her head cupped in her open palm. Because you're you. One hundred percent genuine you. Because I don't know anybody else like you.

What's so special about that? I don't have much of an education, don't own much cept what's in an old trunk. And here you are might be worth a million dollars some day. It's like me competing with that sky up there all a glitter. Somehow we just don't seem to fit.

I'm sorry, she said. About the million dollar comment. It was just an old part of me slipping out. What people have and own isn't what keeps them from fitting. It's who they *are*.

He turned back, supporting his head in similar fashion so they looked like two halves of a statue lying side by side, and looked at her, at the openness of her face, as childlike and innocent as the candleflames reflected in her eyes. I know that, he said. But I also know where I was for six years and who didn't stand in the way of my being there and I just wonder if it hasn't fallen into place in your thinking that your family doesn't care for me.

My family doesn't run my life. Nobody runs my life, not any more.

But they—

Hush up, she said, teasingly, placing a finger on his lips. I don't want to talk about them. She reached behind her head and pulled the ribbon holding her ponytail and her hair fell dark and lustrous around her shoulders and he smelled its sweet fragrance before it curtained around his face as she leaned over and kissed him, her mouth as sweet and clean as her hair, then swung her leg over his and he felt her crotch slide in soft against his. He put an arm around her and pulled her closer and she responded locking her legs even tighter around his. Her breasts were firm against him and further down he could feel himself bulge against her. Every nerve was alive where they touched and through that fusion of cloth and flesh he could feel her heart beating against his, her eyelids against his cheek, her breath a soft roar in his ears, her heat warming him and he lay there afraid to move, afraid if he did everything would stop.

A soft breeze blew now and then whipping the candleflames that were burning low, but none went out. The aroma of the broken earth washed over them and they said nothing, just lay there wrapped in each other listening to the sounds of the night. Doves cooing to one another across the lake. Fish popping the top of the water for insects. Deep bass of frogs, soprano of whippoorwills far off. In the velvety haze of wine everything seemed to expand, yet invade him at the same time.

For the longest nothing was said, neither moved.

Then, she slowly rolled on top of him, encircling his neck with her arms. A hot shiver passed through him and her face, pale in the faint commingling of moon and candle light, came down fast upon him, her mouth wild on his, the rest of her body as hungry, moving against him, stirring within him the same desperate need. Her hands were under his shirt and his in her hair and he felt his body shake, like a loose vibration, a great leaping inside of him, then leave the ground, drift under the control of her hands, her direction, for she knew what to do and he did not, then time and motion ceased.

When it was over, he lay on top of her, softly coupled, desiring once more not to move, prolonging the moment as long as he could, then finally rolled over, his eyes taking in the gloss of silvery outline her body made in the moonlight and his mouth parted to say the words, *Athen, I never*, but thought against it. He'd heard the stories, of parking on country roads, blankets spread in the fields and mattresses rolled out in the beds of pickups, but *Athen, I never*. Confessing to her might mean she'd feel she needed to confess to him. Even if she didn't, he'd see it in her eyes when they looked away. And that was not something he needed to see. Not now. He might tell her some day, when he was ready. When they both were.

She leaned over and kissed him again, her breasts pools of warmth against his skin, pulling herself closer to him and they lay there beneath the still and soundless trees, listening to the remains of the night, its solos and choruses, the beat of its heart.

Lying awake that night in his bed he knew it was wrong. Down deep in blood and bone and sinew he knew it was wrong, yet somehow in that knowing it was wrong, in the very center of that knowing, he knew he was going to do it anyway. And in that shameless knowing it was wrong, his body wanted to remember it all, each moment, each touch, and every word she spoke. But all his mind would allow to come together was the pain-but-not-pain look on her face and the loud cry with it that stilled the night, shook every bird from their roosts and stoppered every creature's voice. Before he trembled and shook and cried out with her. Before heaven and earth collided and the moon and every star funneled through him into her then rose again and took their proper place in the order of things, an image and a sound he would evoke in his mind for years to come, an urgency of desire never before known, nor ever again afterward, of something gained and something lost in the fell swoop of the moment, though of what, he was unsure, when she cried out: NOW, Jo Shelby, take me NOW.

And did he ever.

In the phosphorescent wash of moonlight streaming through the window he wondered what light would guide the way, what future would be revealed. What would happen when she went away to Atlanta, if she did? Would she find someone else? If she didn't and they did get married, what would the wedding be like, the memory of the only one he'd attended with his parents in Drew coming to mind? He guessed it would be in their little Methodist Church in Rome, the one they both grew up in. He let that scene play out in his imagination. People coming from all over, dressed to the nines, asking the ushers to be seated on the bride's side and the ushers telling them the side didn't matter, the groom didn't have one, that thought giving rise to who his best man would be. Where would they live? On whose land? In whose name? Would they have children? Oh, yes, most definitely. Little girls who wore large ribbons in their hair and liked to play dolls and little boys who liked horses. How many? As many as he could afford to take care of. He went back over it all, wondering what he had left out, for something seemed missing. All he wanted to do was get married and have children, that was what a man was supposed to do, that was what had been instilled in him from the day he was born, that was what living and doing right and obeying God's will was all about. But still, something was missing. Maybe it was right there beaming down on him like the moon and he couldn't see it, couldn't see it for the *NOW, Jo Shelby, take me NOW* still beating in his head like a bird trapped in a chimney, until he finally drifted off to sleep.

Next morning they shopped the streets of Clarksdale where she saw a thing or two she liked but nothing struck his fancy. All he seemed to see were places where he'd gone with his parents. The picture show, cafes where they'd eaten, the jewelry store where he watched his father buy his mother a diamond ring for their tenth wedding anniversary. He asked if there wasn't somewhere else they could shop and they drove south on U.S. 51 to Cleveland, a town laid out like Drew with a railroad track down the middle, only larger.

At a downtown department store that was having a fifty percent sale, he purchased a black suit along with a navy blue sport coat, a pair of gray wool slacks, two white shirts and a snappy red and blue-striped tie. Between the money he already had plus the advance Mr Bo gave him he was able to add a pair of black wing-tip lace-up shoes. As a gift, Athen added a shiny black leather belt she said he needed.

That night he wore his new suit and shirt and tie, along with the new belt and black shoes. He checked himself out in the mirror before leaving his apartment, surprised at what a few new clothes could do for a man then tried to remember the last time he'd worn a suit, and couldn't.

Mr Bo let him borrow the truck again and he called on her at the back patio door. She was wearing a red skirt with snappy red heels, a white blouse open at the neck, her long dark hair down and flipped up on her shoulders. As she descended the steps, beneath the shower of light her beauty seemed a thing so very strong, yet so very fragile, so real, yet unreal, sure but unsure. A thing so very Delta.

He grabbed her arm to walk her to the truck but she pulled him away toward her car.

What're we doing. I've got us a ride.

Let's go in my car, she said.

He stopped. How come?

Because I want to. I want you to drive. I've never enjoyed a ride in my own car as a passenger. She was a few steps ahead of him, near the small red convertible, its top down.

He didn't move.

Well, come on. Here, take these, she said, jingling the keys before him with the tips of her fingers. They won't bite you. They're not any different from the ones to that pickup. They go in the same place, turn the same way. Besides it's easier to drive. It's automatic.

Automatic?

You don't have to shift gears. Just turn it on, put the gear in D for Drive and go. They've been around a few years.

You keep forgetting I hadn't.

Sorry.

Only difference is it's a sportscar and if something happened to it while I was driving my life'd be in hock. Besides, I don't have a license yet.

You've been driving Mr Bo's truck without a license. Don't even think about that. We'll be careful.

He settled into his half of the upholstered leather two-seater, let himself get the feel of the steering wheel, the equipment around him, checked out the strange dash with all its many shapes and colors. Feel like this thing might just fly when I turn it on, he said.

She laughed. That's why it's called a Thunderbird.

He put the key into the ignition, turned it, pressed his foot gently on the accelerator and felt the smooth power come alive and purr beneath him.

Wait just a minute before you fly, she said, wrapping a scarf around her hair and tying it tightly under her delicate chin. Now.

He steered the car carefully down the drive, through the pillared gates and into the open stretches of the night, the cool wind whipping around them as though generated by the vehicle itself, the flow of the motor under his foot like something issuing forth, the highway something he was laying down as he went. She turned on the radio. They listened to Elvis and Bill Haley and the Comets and Fats Domino and Muddy Waters. But it was Chuck Berry singing a tune called Maybellene that got Jo Shelby to nodding his head up and down to the rhythm and playing the steering wheel with his hands like a drum.

You act like you never heard rock 'n roll, she said loudly into the wind.

I've heard it all right, he turned to her and shouted back. Just the first time I felt it.

Inside, the Ruleville Club looked like one huge log cabin, dark exposed beams and rafters vaulting upward, a large open dining area surrounded by smaller rooms for private parties, massive stone fireplace centering one wall, a roaring fire licking through four-foot logs. The place was crowded and noisy but seemed to hush as they entered, grow quieter still as they were led to their table. This was where his father would not take his mother, he thought as he followed the waiter and Athen. This was a wall he ... they ... were kicking down.

The waiter led them toward a corner table for two at the back.

He extended a hand to pull her chair out for her, but the waiter beat him to it. Once they were seated the subdued hum of voices picked back up, as though the interruption had been of little consequence, a minor distraction to their self-indulged worlds of talk. But the craned necks and turned heads, the hundred pairs of eyes drawing a bead on them, suggested otherwise.

He opened his menu, looked at her over the top. I had a man tell me not long ago I had spunk, he said.

And? she said.

I don't know what spunk plus spunk equals, but I think we may just find out.

I thought we just did, she said, smiling. Wonder how many jaws locked up?

I can't count that high, he said with a chuckle. But there's two sets of em over there hadn't closed yet. Look like they could chop a ten-penny nail in two.

Who's that?

Your brothers. Behind you. Three tables over.

She glanced back over her shoulder, flipped a quick wave of her hand at Josh and Jake and their wives then looked back at her menu. Don't be bothered by them. They still think they need to look after their little sis.

Guess they want a closer look. They're headed this way.

They wore plaid sport coats and button-down white shirts with loud ties and their eyes had an ass-whippin, alcohol-glazed design about them as they simultaneously bent down and kissed their sister on each cheek, then stood grinning crooked at him.

So, lil' Sis, you takin the boy out on the town tonight, Jake said, the words sliding sluggish from his mouth on heavy fumes of bourbon that crossed the table to Jo Shelby. He hoped the single candle burning in the middle didn't flare to the ceiling. He kept his eyes on his menu, scooted his chair back slightly. He moved one hand behind his back and felt the distance from the walls where they joined, how much room he had behind him.

Jake, go sit down, Athen said, rolling her eyes angrily at him. What I do is none of your business.

Josh reached over, brought his hand down in a loud slap on the table in front of Jo Shelby. I'd say business is business and if you knew what Jo boy there was tryin to do with ours, which is yours, too, you might be just a tad upset. Aint that right Jo boy?

If their entrance had brought a slight lull to the dissonant babble of tables, Josh's action shut it down to a murmur, so quiet the flames in the fireplace sounded like cap guns going off and the clinking of silverware around the room like a dull tuneless choir of bells.

Jo Shelby met his corrupt grin with a hard look over the top of the menu. The name's Jo Shelby.

Now, I say it's Jo boy, boy. Josh was leaning over the table now, his eyes and breath telling the tale of his early evening.

Athen slapped her napkin on the table. Josh, shut up. Y'all go back to your table. You're making a spectacle.

Sorry, Sis, but you the one makin the spectacle, Jake said. Traipsin in here like the Maid of Cotton with Bo Stevens' hired hand.

Jo Shelby had propped his menu in front of him to shield his hands, maneuvered the wooden-handled fork and steak knife behind it. Believe you fellers need to do what the lady says, he said glowering at them over his propped menu, his voice low and hard. Or you won't believe what's gonna happen next.

Beside Athen they stood, both leaning over, heads lolling, their ties spilling out of their open coats onto the table like streams of paint down a wall onto a floor.

Well lookie here, said Josh, leaning over further, his smeared alcoholic grin near a drool. Jo boy here's gittin tough.

Yeah, Jake said. We gotta talk to lil Sis bout her taste, don't we now?

Some folks' taste is just in their mouth, Jo Shelby said. He stood up and pushed his chair back and in a swift singular motion brandished knife and fork in the air bringing them down onto the ties, impaling them to the soft pine tabletop.

Son of a bitch, Josh and Jake screamed together.

Come on, Athen, Jo Shelby said in a low firm voice.

They eased from the table and hand in hand, eyes straight ahead, threaded their way through the gauntlet of astonished faces, an air of deliberation about them, oblivious to the screaming profanities behind them, Josh and Jake's cries still audible in the cool night air as Jo Shelby cranked the car and they sped off, the Thunderbird spraying gravel for fifty yards until they hit the highway.

Where we going? Athen shouted at him, trying to get her scarf on.

Don't know. He looked at her and grinned and she put her hands over her mouth and began laughing.

I would've stayed and fought em but that would've made us part of the spectacle.

She was still laughing, doubled up in her seat like she was having a fit.

It wasn't that damn funny, he said. I could've gotten my butt beat. May still.

It was ... She was trying to talk between spasms ... It was funny ... but what makes it funnier ... is mama hates those ties ... and their wives do, too.

He began laughing with her, all the way to the drive-in in Drew.

They ordered Bar-B-Q sandwiches and French fries and Cokes, sat in the car and ate, laughing still at what had happened, Athen not content to let it rest, having to retell it over and over until she finally wore it out as the evening wound down.

They drove home in silence, the engine roaring into the dark, the only other sounds the wind and whining tires sucking up the road, the radio, the songs feeding his thoughts, telling his history. Frank Sinatra Singing The Blues and Fats Domino Aint That A Shame. Somebody named J. P. Morgan taking The Longest Walk. It got better with Moments To Remember and Only You, adding a little romance to the open-air night, giving rise to thoughts of what they'd do next, if they'd repeat the night before, that memory growing between his legs as he pulled into the long drive to the house and the something sisters started singing Something's Gotta Give and she turned to him and said, Jo Shelby, what *were* Jake and Josh talking about, about you and our business?

* * *

He lay awake that night replaying the evening in his mind, trying to figure out what went wrong, how it could have gone downhill so fast after feeling so good the night before, when she pulled him into her and a sweet lightening struck between them. He told her the history of the house and the land as he knew it, as it had been passed down from family to family. He told her of his father's failed attempts at the chancery clerk's office. He told her of his discovery in Mexico on his return trip, finding the graves and the dates on the markers, that the old Colonel was still alive in Mexico when the property switched hands, that his father's suspicion had been right. Foster didn't have the right to sell the land, much less gamble it away. He told her that there was probably an old deed or will somewhere saying all that. He told her all he wanted was what was fair and square, that he owed that to his daddy and his before him and so on, that he didn't want to sue anybody, omitting he'd seen an attorney in Drew. With all she'd said about the Delta—how she didn't like living there, didn't want to be like the people who lived there, wished she hadn't even been born there—surely she'd understand.

He told her all that while they were standing on the patio at the kitchen door, her eyes flaring, blazing out of sockets suddenly turned pale, as if that was where the blood was shocked first before it began leaving her face. She stood there glaring at him beneath the bulb above the doorway, her face blanched in the single bright light, her lips quivering, shoulders trembling. For a moment he thought she might roll her eyes and pass out right there on the stoop, then the blood started coming back, as quickly as it had drained, a crimson shade moving up her face, over-riding her rouge and lipstick and anything else that was supposed to make her look prettier so that all he saw was a fierce and ugly anger hanging in the white bright light as if suspended in it. When she finally spoke all she said was, That's just it, Jo Shelby Ferguson. You're the one who doesn't understand. You haven't heard anything I've said then she opened the door and with a single bang was gone behind it.

As best he could remember, lying there in bars of quarter moon streaming through the slatted blinds, that was the way it went. He continued obsessing on what had happened, all that was said, hadn't been said, trying to fix on a look or a word or a phrase, something for his thinking to grab and hold on to. But the only constant in the wheeling spiral of thoughts, that kept coming around and around like a bully on a merry-go-round, was that her mama and daddy were coming back from Memphis. When they heard what happened at the Ruleville Club that would be fat in a fire already burning out of control.

He awoke later on, unsure why. He didn't need to go to the bathroom and he hadn't heard anything. The clock by the bed said three-thirty. Then came light taps from the door downstairs. Athen must have had a change of heart and driven over to apologize, stomping off the way she did, not even saying goodnight. That wasn't like her, leaving like that, slamming the door. He turned on the lamp and stepped into the suit pants he'd worn, pulled them up over his pajama bottoms so the top hung loose over his waist. He thought of putting his shoes on, then not. He'd just invite her up. Mr Bo and Miss Floy wouldn't mind.

Descending the steps, he heard the taps again, the same impatience behind them. He opened the door and looked around, saw no one. He stepped out onto the concrete stoop to get a better look and a strong hand grabbed his neck from behind while another crammed a rag down his mouth. Something rough and dark like a wool sheath shuttered violently over his head and the world went black. Then a drunken voice from the dark said, we gonna have us a real necktie party.

He was kicking and flailing the air with his arms, trying to free himself, trying to holler though the rag. But there were two of them and one of him and within seconds they had his arms pinned and tied behind his back and he was thrown headfirst into the rear of a pickup, his head banging hard on the metallic bed, his face burning across the coarse material of the hood which he'd figured was a croker sack, for it had that smell of rotten potatoes. He heard the doors slam, then sick laughter from the cab as the motor turned over and the truck headed down the smooth drive and onto the pot-holed macadam and in short time was bouncing over a rough crop road. Rolling and slamming about in the sharp turns, he lost any since of direction.

He tried to work his hands free but his wrists were tied tightly with hemp rope and the more he struggled the more they sawed against his skin and burned. What machinations their evil minds had concocted he could only imagine, but surely not a lynching. Even drunk, they wouldn't kill him. Maybe rough him up some, teach him a lesson, but not kill him. They'd shot and killed a fawn though, just for fun, tender venison on the table an afterthought. The truck rocked on, veering sharply right and left, then right again, taking them deeper into the maze of fields, away from lights and sounds. Away from help.

Then they stopped.

He waited. Listened.

Doors croaked opened, slammed shut, the sounds amplified through the dark. Then the tailgate clanged down. Rough hands gripped his ankles and dragged him out.

He said nothing. That was one thing he had learned in prison, American or Mexican. Talking invited pain.

They said nothing as they stood him up.

He knew only what he could feel and hear. The hard cool ground beneath his bare feet. Footsteps walking away from him. Laughter. Doors slamming. Then the sound of the motor revving.

He stood still, fearing they might run him down. They'd do that drunk, maybe even sober. They were men without consciences. The motor was still loud then it faded. He listened to its sputtering drone, followed its direction until it blended with the other faint murmurs percolating through the night.

He calculated his options, the one or two he had. His feet were not shackled. He wasn't blindfolded. If he could just get the sack off his head he could see, get a step up on the situation. He knelt onto the ground then lay on his back. Using the ground as a pincer to hold the sack he began working his body, scooting forward, backing up, scooting forward again, repeating the procedure until his head cleared the sack and he was able to breathe something besides rank potatoes and his own recycled breath. He rolled upright on his knees. He placed one foot behind the other, pushed himself up, stood, looked around. The sky bowled over him like something peppered with brilliance. The half-moon burned bright as though full and he wondered about the arithmetic of light, how half of something shining could equal its whole, then quickly thanked the heavens he had what he had, a means to find his way home.

Far to the south he could see the lights of the penitentiary, which meant they'd dropped him at the northern most sector of the Patrick property, north of the Rome-Clarksdale macadam highway, as far as he could be from the Stevens line. Which meant he wasn't lost, just a few miles from home, a good hike ahead of him. Thank the Lord he wasn't near the prison line. Barefooted and wearing a striped pajama top with his hands tired behind his back he'd be shot on sight as an escapee, no questions asked.

He needed to get the rag out of his mouth. It tasted like disinfectant and backed his tongue against his throat so he gagged every time he swallowed. He began working his tongue, purchasing some space, then thrusting the tongue against the wad, shoving on it like it was some boulder that required all a man's might, feeling the blood vessels across his forward and down his temples engorge and throb until the wad finally broke loose and he spit it out, hoping whatever it had on it wouldn't make him sick.

No way to get his hands freed unless he could find something sharp. A disk blade would do. Weather permitting, workers occasionally parked tractors in the field so they could start up where they left off the next morning. His father had even found keys left in them. Jo Shelby scanned the horizon for the silhouette of one but all he could see was a ring of dark treeline encircling the lighter horizon like a stain. He started walking, following the crop road that ribboned before him, its tracks silver in the moonlight, patinaed smooth by years of truck and tractor tires and the constant patter of bare black feet.

He wasn't sure his exact location, but by the lights of the penitentiary and position of the moon and north star, he knew the direction he needed to go. Southwest. At least he knew that. The rest was simple geometry. Keep the penitentiary lights due south. Follow the hypotenuse toward the setting moon. Sooner or later he'd hit the macadam road because this was the Delta, where a man could lose a lot of things but had to be damn near demented to lose his way. Once he hit the macadam road help might come along. His feet would at least have a smoother surface to the Stevens'. It would just take time, a couple of hours, maybe longer.

It was not yet dawn when he stumbled into the Stevens' compound, his hands still bound behind him. His wrists were rubbed raw, probably bleeding. His feet sore and hurting from rocks stumbled on and snagged along the way. He thought of ringing the doorbell with his head or banging it against the door, then thought again. No need getting Mr Bo and Miss Floy all involved. He made his way instead to the tractor shed.

The plow blades were low off the ground but by squatting and leaning against one, purchasing leverage with his feet, he commenced the up-and-down sawing movement needed to free him. The ropes were quarter inch hemp at least, so it took a while. His legs ached into his thighs and down his shins and he had to stop every few minutes, but he kept on until the last tether snapped and his hands were free and he could caress his wrists.

He kept the rope, in case he'd need it later, for what reason he wasn't sure. Just seemed the thing to do. He crawled up the steps of the garage apartment, removed his clothes and fell into bed, his lids clapping shut like weights over his eyes.

He awoke to a slash of sunlight raking his eyes, birds chirping madly away outside the window above him, the sound of a car motor turning over, then a familiar muffled roar. He crawled from the bed in time to glimpse the rear of the Thunderbird leave the drive and disappear behind the hedge, its throaty drone fading down the road. He turned from the window and looked at the clock by the bed. Two-thirty.

Damn, he whispered to himself. Afternoon.

He tried to hurry but his body wouldn't let him. It hurt just putting on a shirt. He couldn't step into a pair of jeans. He had to sit on the side of the bed and pull them on. His feet were too sore for shoes so he went without them.

By the time he'd rung the Stevens' doorbell there was already one ringing in his head, from the pain he guessed he aggravated in the short distance.

Good Lord, Jo Shelby! What happened to you? Miss Floy said, opening the door. We wondered if you were all right when you didn't come down to ride to church with us. Look at your feet and wrists. Her eyes were alarms, the irises tiny brown balls ringing against the expanding whites.

Oh, that, he said looking down innocently at his wrists ringed raspberry red and raw and his feet scuffed and scraped, blood-encrusted and dust-congealed along the sides, a purple hull of skin over a big toe where he'd stumped it. He couldn't think of anything to say. Of all the planning he'd done on the long walk back, he hadn't given thought to his wounds, the story to go with them.

Well, come on in. You need some doctoring up.

He sat in the den while she scurried around the kitchen opening and shutting drawers, then returned carrying a tray rattling with bottles of Mercurochrome and iodine and rubbing alcohol along with wads of cotton and gauze and Band-Aids, half a drug store it seemed. All she needed was a little white hat and white stockings and rubber-soled white shoes to say Nurse Floy.

Mr Bo knocked on the door a few times but you never answered, she said, opening the bottle of rubbing alcohol, the smell invading the room like a hospital had just blown in.

I was asleep.

Some sleep, she said dousing alcohol on a wad of cotton. This is going to sting.

Yessum. He clenched his teeth and flinched as she gently dabbed at first, then swabbed around his wrist.

What did happen to you? She looked directly into his eyes, the mother's look that always knows more.

I'd kindly rather not say.

That's fine she said, narrowing not-fine eyes as she dabbed and swabbed the other wrist, as he clenched his teeth and flinched again. But Mr Bo won't let you off that easy.

Where's he?

He's down feeding the horses. But he'll be back shortly then I'm going to turn you over to him. She smiled when she said it, but it was a tight smile, an I-don't-mean-business tight smile.

They sat juxtaposed in silence, he in the chair and she on the ottoman nursing him, hurting him gently with care, the way his mama would. With her head down, from that angle she even looked like his mama, the brown hair soft as down.

All those fights you told us about in Mexico?

Yessum?

Who took care of you down there, doctored you up after those? she said, a meddlesome tone in her voice.

He told her of Ramon, the old political prisoner in Matamoras, how he patched him up with what medical supplies Athen had put in his knapsack before he left. He told about his wife, Senora Rosario in Monterrey, the different manner in which she nursed him, the help she rendered. He told about Blanche King, the owner of the Bella Vista Hotel In Cuernavaca, of her special knowledge of his family and how she offered refuge to him after his money had been stolen. He told her of Senora Moncada, her treatment of him in like manner when he was beaten and almost hanged in her front yard. As he spoke Miss Floy continued swabbing and bandaging, glancing up at him with an uncertain eye as he talked. Then he stopped, as one stops when he's saving the best to last.

There is more, she said. It was not a question.

Yessum. There's those. Then there's Carmen.

She was guiding a pair of scissors along a strip of tape and she stopped. Carmen, she said, cocking her head to one side as if the sound just funneled into her ear needed an extra nudge. What a pretty name. It's the name of an opera. Mr Bo and I saw it when it came to Memphis a few years ago.

Operas are kinda like plays, aren't they?

Yes. Only they have music and elaborate settings. People dress up in costumes and sing their parts. She'd let go the scissors and was moving her arms dramatically in the air. They are gorgeous productions.

Carmen's an opera, then, he said smiling.

Miss Floy laughed. Well, I hope she's not like the Carmen in *that* opera.

Why's that?

In the story Carmen is a very beautiful gypsy, a wanderer. She dances around men, throws flowers to them, seduces them. They fight over her. She flits about causing trouble, kind of like a gypsy moth.

Nome. This Carmen's not like that.

She watched him as he said it, with eyes no longer speculative. The way you said that, she must be special, she said.

Yessum, she's special all right. He told of her care and treatment of him, her knowledge of Mexico City, of its museums and libraries that helped in locating the lost remnants of his family, letting slip the two weeks spent with her during Christmas on his return journey.

You were right, Miss Floy said when he finished.

How's that?

She's not like the Carmen in the opera. If she'd been like that Carmen, you would not have come back.

He didn't tell her his next thought as she put the finishing touches on the last bandage.

There, she said, tapping his knee with her finger. Not good as new, but that ought to do you for a while.

Mr Bo came through the door in a huff, complaining loudly about one of the horses kicking him then he looked over and saw nurse and patient.

What the—Jo Shelby, what the hell happened to you?

He made them commit to secrecy before telling the story, backing up to the Ruleville Club because, with half the Delta elite looking on, they'd surely hear that part.

So you're pretty sure it was Josh and Jake, Mr Bo said, his face red as sunset.

I'm sure it was. I could hear em talking. I'd know those voices anywhere.

And they came on my—he speared his chest with a finger—on my property and took you. By damn, that's trespassing. It's kidnapping and trespassing.

Now Bo, don't go getting your blood pressure up, Miss Floy said. You know what Dr. Bostwick said.

I damn sure do and the best way to get it down is call Sheriff Posey.

You promised Jo Shelby you'd say nothing about this, she said sternly to him.

Thank you ma'am, Jo Shelby said, nodding at her.

Mr Bo blew breath through his nose then got up and started pacing.

Athen was here not long ago, Miss Floy said.

Did you talk to her? Jo Shelby said.

No. I saw her through the kitchen window. Wasn't playing close attention. I saw her drive in and walk over to the apartment, Next thing I knew, she was driving away.

I knew y'all were friends, Mr Bo said, stopping his pacing. But didn't realize you were serious.

Don't reckon we are anymore, Jo Shelby said.

How come? Mr Bo said, still standing in one place.

Bo, that's none of our business, Miss Floy said.

He started pacing again.

He didn't see the note going out but he wasn't looking. Returning through the apartment door he saw it on the bottom step against the wall, a white square envelope, unsealed, the flap tucked inside, TO JO SHELBY scrawled in blue ink across the front. He unfolded the flap, pulled out three sheets, and began reading.

Dear Jo Shelby,

I knocked on your door several times so we could talk but you wouldn't come down.

I'm sorry I walked away last night the way I did but I couldn't believe what I was hearing.

It's all still very painful for me. Maybe it's because of where I am with my life and where you are with yours and the fact they're not in the same place, though I had thought they were.

Maybe it's because of our different worlds and what we've learned, or not learned from them.

Maybe it's because I thought I knew you, then suddenly wondered if I did or not. Maybe it's because I don't care what happened a hundred years ago and

you do. All I know is you're all caught up with that and I'm not and don't in-
tend to be. And it took your telling me your plan, as you called it, to open my
eyes. We both need some time, time to think and decide where our lives are re-
ally going.

I'm not sure when I'll be home again, maybe Easter.

Maybe we can talk then. Regardless of what happens, we will always be
friends. We've known and cared for each other too long to throw that away.

Athen

He stood in the stairwell breathing heavily, his lungs deflating as though assaulted by a single blow and suddenly not enough air in the world to sustain him, his whole body abruptly nothing but heartbeat and breathing struggling against each other. He remembered the day he was marched into a cell and the heavy door clanged shut behind him, that sound now ushered up by memory. Then it faded and all he could hear were the letter's thin pages rattling dryly in his hand.

He stood there, trying to put a name on the feeling washing over him. After all he'd been through, it sure to God had to be one not yet known or named. Maybe it was just the same fear that strikes any man when he risks loving a woman and she conjures up some lunacy to cancel it out, that thought bringing on the second feeling riding the tail of the first. He brought the trembling pages to his eyes and read them again, the long list of maybes. Then her name. Just her name.

He smacked his hands together, crumbling the two sheets and envelop into a small wad, squeezing them as if by sheer force he could make them disappear, then jammed the small compacted ball into his jeans pocket and climbed the dusky stairs. A man can't be down and mad at the same time, his father once told him, that if his life ever came to choosing one or the other, he could live off mad. Nothing lived off the blues except colored folks. And he didn't call that living.

He sat in his room on his bed, rereading the note and thinking. She loved him because of who he was she'd said that night by the lake and now just signed her name. Because of where his life was now, where he came from, that hundred years she wanted no part of. She hadn't taken the love back, just not-said it, like it was still there in the not-there, something she'd come this far with, wasn't sure what to do with, but didn't want to get rid of. The more he thought about that the more his thinking turned inward. *You're not the only one in this world who's got a long story, Jo Shelby Ferguson.* She'd grown up in one prison while he was serving time in another, she'd said. Her mama and daddy didn't own her anymore, she'd said. Nobody did, she'd said. *I don't intend to spend the rest of my life in this prison.* He should have jumped in the air and cheered when she said it, should've hugged and kissed and congratulated her. But he sat there like a knot on a log feeling a cold lonely loss, then hammered her with his own selfish questions. Blood sure enough does run thicker than water and theirs were two rivers running in opposite directions. She said maybe things would change. Maybe.

He felt an aloneness he'd never before known, one worse than prison. In prison you were lonely because of three walls and a grilled door and a patrol of khaki-clothed shot-gun-toting guards that told you why you were lonely. Because you couldn't get out and nothing could get in and it was all simple fact and understandable. Now he was out and something was rushing in, pushing on him, crowding around his heart and squeezing his stomach. He wondered what he'd do the rest of the day.

He didn't have a telephone so he couldn't call her. He didn't have a car so he couldn't drive to Oxford. Fact was, he didn't have diddly. He might as well put his shoes on, walk to the penitentiary line and announce to the guards, here I am, Johnny come home. The penitentiary at least had company, and rules he understood.

The next day he worked hurt, rode a tractor eight to five, every bounce in the metal seat paining his body like sprays of birdshot riddling his buttocks. He thought about what he was doing. Middlebusting. Busting up where something had grown and died, throwing the dirt one way, then the other. That was about right, what his life had been, one busted right down the middle, part thrown one way, part another. When he died he'd even go to that Great Middlebuster in the sky who separates the wheat from the chaff, the goats from the sheep. He thought about that a while, God having to middlebust, too, before He could plant again.

He thought about Mr Doom at the courthouse, the man who ratted on him, and how he was going to deal with him. He needed to get back to lawyer Darden but that would take a half a day and he hadn't been working long enough for more time off. He could pretend he was sick. When a hired hand got sick on Mr Pat's place they just took you to the doctor in Drew or the hospital in Ruleville. If it was the hospital, you got left until you were well, then they brought you back, the only consolation being Mr Pat paid the bills. If he got sick at the Stevens he'd have Miss Floy as a nurse again and be bedridden under her watchful eye. He could hope and pray for rain, heavy enough to keep them out of the fields. His father liked those days. He'd always come in the house, take off his boots and read, work a crossword puzzle, nap. The rainy days that give a man a chance to catch up on his life. He'd think about that, pray for a rainy day.

Row after row, turnaround after turnaround, he went over everything again in his mind. He didn't want the big house and all the buildings that went with it. He didn't want all the machinery and all the equipment. He didn't want the barn and the horses, any of the cars or pickups. He didn't want to fire the new foreman and make his family move out of the house he was raised in. He didn't want any of that. He'd come back for two things and two things only. Athen and the land title rectified, two pieces that fit snuggly in his mind when he left Mexico and a senorita who thought he hung the moon and now banged wildly against each other like a child trying to put square peg in a round hole.

He came to a turnaround and wheeled the tractor in ruts made by another the season before and kept on plowing but no other thoughts came to him, none that would solve the puzzle. He remembered a movie he'd seen once about World War II, some soldiers picking their way across a mine field and decided that was where he was and he'd have to just pick his way through this one and hope nothing or nobody got blown up.

The pop, pop, popping of the tractor hammered in his ears and he wished he were behind a team of quiet mules. There had to be a way out. He knew if he prayed about it, thought long and hard enough, he would see it. Being patient hadn't let him down in the past. If nothing else, it kept hope alive. Blessed are those who wait upon the Lord, his mama would read to him from her Bible, calling out the name of the book and verse before she read. One night it might come from Psalms, another night Isaiah, the next Job and so on. From Genesis to Revelation waiting on the Lord was there. As if that was the whole Bible summed up, what religion was really all about. His daddy telling him, too, when something bad happened and didn't go his way, that it would pass, then quoting his favorite scripture: *And it came to pass.* As if time was God's other name and if you just hung around long enough He'd come to you. Not to heal your pain, but bless you for outlasting it. That was the hard part. Waiting for the blessing.

III

Time was when time was something he didn't count, when it was one long stretch of days and nights running together and running nowhere, all one circular process, without division or demarcation, simply there, spinning, stuck in one place like a period, not laid out like a sentence, though that's what they called what he was doing. He was serving time and that was his sentence but he lived in the no-time, in the there-ness, not knowing or caring when and where he was in it because when and where were words long gone. The only word that mattered was *there*. Then he got out and was still not counting because he'd been in prison so long his mind had forgotten how or been worn down to just breathing second to second or just didn't care because there was nothing to get out for. Then she said she loved him, then not-said it and he began counting—the hours, days, she didn't come home.

He thought she'd call after a few days, surely a week. It was not a harsh note. It said they were still friends and would talk again. He thought surely there'd be a note on his door or Miss Floy would holler at him from the backdoor and tell him she was on the phone. They'd had spats growing up, pouts that followed. He remembered once pushing her into a creek. He was fifteen and she was eleven. She was wearing a plain white T-shirt and cut-off bluejean shorts ragged around the bottom. When she came out of the water her hair was gooey and flopped over her face like an entanglement of mustard greens. Her long legs, no longer bony but not fully fleshed out either, were slicked over with a muddy gunk the same color of her hair. But all his eyes could focus on was the wet T-shirt sticking to her skin and the small pointed breasts shining through it like little ripened plums and he lay awake nights dreaming about them. She didn't speak to him for several days, wouldn't even come outside. A few weeks later, she got even by coaxing him into the barn loft then pulling the ladder away, leaving him stranded among bales of hay in a scratchy sweltering heat, for hours it seemed, until his mother heard his calls and came to the rescue. He didn't speak to her for over a week. But they'd always get back together, manage it in a way that required simple arithmetic, nothing taken away or given up, no sacrifice or confession, apology or forgiveness. He'd hit a ball into her yard where she was pretending to ignore him and she'd eventually throw it back. He'd hit it again and she'd throw it back again and soon the bases were set, a score running. Or she'd leave a mysterious note along the unmarked boundary of their yards, near the slide or the swing set. He'd take it and leave one in its place. Within days there'd be a new postal service for the Patrick plantation, postmistress and postman busy getting out the mail, delivering it to any and everybody that'd play along with their new business. They always worked out their problems, came around to each other in that small world of childhood where the next playmates were miles away and if you didn't want to be lonely and wanted someone to play with you learned to make up, that it didn't hurt and didn't cost anything and got you out of the lives of grownups who'd forgotten all that.

He'd written a letter she hadn't answered. Addressed it Athen Patrick, Chi O House, University of Mississippi. He'd tried calling her sorority house twice from pay phones he was able to find. Each time, lacquered-over girlish voices answered saying she wasn't in, could they take a message. All he could do was leave his name, say he'd called. She knew where he was, how to reach him.

Late one afternoon he walked down the road from the Stevens' to Sissy's place, a small shanty with missing boards and sagging eaves and broken windows, something the next good storm might blow over. He recalled those storms from the west, purple walls of night that blotted out the sky and sent raging winds ahead of them, blasts of dust and grit, some so fierce they knocked down trees and blew over sheds, toppled barns and lifted house frames from their foundations, carried cars and refrigerators and sometimes people miles from where they'd been and he wondered if that was why the Delta was flat. Not because of the timeless work of the rivers but what those furies could level in a handful of seconds. He thought of another, too, he saw coming. Not one of wind and rain, though folks would've wished it had been, but one that would rearrange the whole Delta, shake it from top to bottom. He was up for the ride, his thinking having traveled that far from his youth. It was the people around him he wondered about. They didn't even see it coming.

Her name was Cassie Mae Longest. She'd been the Patricks' maid for as long as he could remember. Like his daddy and mama, she came with the land. Which meant her family, like his, were there long before the Patricks. Which made her the closest of kin he had on the American side, even if she was colored. His mama told him once she was his black mammy and he was to obey her as if she was his own blood.

She lived in the shot-gun shack with her husband and children. Jo Shelby never knew exactly how many. Trying to count them one day he ran out of fingers. Whenever he passed the small clapboard dwelling he wondered how they all fit into it. He asked his daddy one day and his daddy said folks just fit in where they have to then tilted his head slightly downward with his eyes lowered, which always conveyed the meaning there was more to what he said than what he said.

He'd always wondered how Sissy did it, took care of one family perfectly capable of caring for themselves then walk two miles home to take care of another that needed her like a body needs air. And she always walked, coming and going, too proud to let the Patricks transport her, he guessed, if they even offered. He figured up the distance, four miles total every day, Sundays included, the time it took to walk the distance and what all she had to do when she got home and figured she got four hours sleep each night, if that. She ought to be on the front of magazines with a big S across her front: Superwoman.

She was rocking on the front porch beside Marvin her husband, their children milling all about them. She saw Jo Shelby approaching and hollered SCRAM! and they exploded around the corners of the dog-trot house. Except Marvin, who snuck through the front door like he was leaving a crime.

Have a seat in Marvin's chair, she said to Jo Shelby and he did. They sat and rocked together, gazed out over the land and talked at first of families. Of his that was gone. Of hers that was ever present and ever troubled but, Lord Jesus be praised, ever blessed and loved. She'd only gotten bits and pieces from Athen's retelling to her parents and wanted to know more about his trip to Mexico.

He told the story again. Sissy ooohed and aaahed and Lawd-a-mercied. When he'd finished, her exclamations sighed on in the still dusk air, as if she was retelling it all to herself, as if it had become a story all her own, one she needed to whisper once more.

Then she stopped rocking and looked at him, with eyes that seemed to hurt, like eyes that have been too long at the sun. Mister Jo Shelby, what I don't understand is why you even come back here, way Mr Pat done you and all.

He stopped rocking, too, looked into the hurt eyes boring into him and thought about the question he'd been asking himself. Fact is, Sissy, that just may be the reason why. I wasn't going to be run off. He almost added, because it was mine in the first place, but stopped himself.

That don't make much sense, not after what you just tole me.

How come you're not up and gone to Chicago, like a lot of your people? he said.

She'd started back rocking then stopped again. Cause of all them chil'ren you seen. Aint enough room for them in Chicargo.

They rocked on in the shared silence, broken only by the rockers popping and groaning across the warped boards, the occasional shriek of a child out back. Then:

That some story, she said, turning and looking at him. But you aint tole it all. Her eyes were strong, unblinking, like his mother's when she knew something was bothering him.

What do you mean?

I aint knowed you all yo life for nothing.

He told her the real reason he'd come to see her and commenced telling her about him and Athen, starting back when they were children growing up on the plantation. Then they were no longer children and their feelings for each other started changing. Not long after that, he went to prison.

I know bout all that, she said. Watched you young'uns since y'all both knee-high a grasshopper. Seen it all a comin.

Seen what comin?

What you tellin me. Go on.

He told her about their short time together since his return from Mexico, of their shared affection, their love for each other, steering clear of the picnic and the evening by the lake. How it all seemed to be going somewhere, then suddenly stopped. He expected her to stop rocking and say something back but she did neither.

He kept talking. He told her about the shopping trip and the incident at the Ruleville Club, carefully omitting his abduction. Of the letter Athen left at the Stevens' and its contents, the phone calls he'd made, messages left, the letter he'd sent. And I haven't heard as much as a peep, he said, slapping the arm of the rocker with his hand.

Sissy stopped rocking and looked at him. Now I remember that mornin. Miss Athen mighty upset.

He stopped rocking. What'd she say?

Somethin bout you bein thick-headed. That what she say. Not to me. What she say to herself whilst she eatin her breakfast.

That all she said?

That it. But both you young uns thick-headed as mules.

He thought of the comparison a moment then let it go.

They rocked. A car drove by, its wheels veering onto the shoulder and throwing gravel as the lone driver's hands pulled with his eyes at the different colors rocking side-by-side, then corrected itself back onto the macadam.

What's this thing you plannin?

Not sure right now. That's what I'm working on.

Not talking bout Miss Athen. What she say you say in that letter.

He recapitulated the history of the land, his discovery in Mexico, that the land still legally belonged to his family and all he wanted to do was set the record straight.

She stopped rocking before he finished, scooted forward and planted both bare feet on the porch planking then pivoted her large bulk on an elbow so she was almost side-ways in the chair and drove a hard look straight into his eyes.

Set the record straight. I say, set the record straight. Her astonished eyes were enlarged, red-veined whites invading her face.

Yessum. That's what I said, what I aim to do.

Like you the onlyst one needs to set a record straight, she grunted, continued glaring at him, her face suddenly perspiring, her breathing heavy, as though expanding and contracting through the bulging eyes.

Naw now. I know—

You know. You don't know didley bout settin no record straight, Mister Jo Shelby Ferguson.

I'm sorry. Didn't mean to upset you.

Her face calmed but she was still turned in the chair and looking at him, a look that wasn't through laying down its points. Aint upsettin Ole Sissy. I done learned upset, done taken upset into my bosom and nourished it like a chile. But you, young un, you fixin to sho nough start sumpin now, she said, the whites of her eyes expanding again. And you aint got no inklin why that girl mad?

Guess cause it's her daddy's land.

That be's part.

What's the rest?

That between you and Miss Athen. I ain't gittin into all that. Might be cause she don't want you hurt. She pivoted around in her chair, as though she was finished, then turned back again. But I'll say this, Mister Jo Shelby. You lissen to Sissy. Her eyes were glistening and pushing forward again as if driving ahead of them the truth they conveyed. Now Miss Athen she a pretty thing, a pretty spoilt thing.

I know that. But not like her mama and daddy spoiled Josh and Jake.

Naw sir, she said, still sitting in that twisted contortion that defied movement. Not like them two. They special cases. They been spoilt by sumpin else, by the devil hisself.

And she's not spoiled like the rest of them, neither, he said. Told me growing up in her house was worse than the prison I was in.

Lemme finish, she said. She talking bout more 'n the house. Most of the white womenfolk down here, they spoilt darlins, Delta darlins, livin in their big houses, drivin their big cars, suckin up life like they was drinkin from a glass didn't have no bottom. An' once they gits the Delta darlin in em, they don't never lose it, mainly cause they don't know they got it to lose in the first place. If you know what I mean.

Yessum. I think I do.

All ceptin Miss Athen. Sissy been watchin her, watching what she do, lissenin to what she say to her mama and her daddy. She spoilt, got the darlin in her all right, mind you. No mistakin that. But what set her off from them others is she know she got it. She leaned further over the arm of the chair and narrowed her eyes sharply to make the additional point. And she don't want it.

She moved to turn around then swung her face back on him. An' I ain't sayin it's all Mister and Miss Pat's doin's neither.

Whose is it then?

It aint no who. You looking at it, she said, reshaping her body to the chair so she was sitting erect and facing once again the land. That why she mad. Yes sir, I seen it a comin. Ole Sissy seen it a comin. And it's a whole lot more 'n that house 'n Mister and Miss Pat. A whole lot more. It be this whole Delta.

He kept at his job, tried to stay busy, whatever Mr Bo had for him to do, mostly riding a tractor dragging down the rows he'd hipped up with the middlebuster, getting them ready for planting. Occasionally he'd take a pickup into Drew to buy a machine part or feed for the horses, pick up an item for Miss Floy. Each time he stopped by Mr Darden's office and each time the old attorney was out. The young lady named Mary Lou told him each time the papers were ready and he told her each time he wasn't, that he needed to talk to lawyer Darden first, that he'd just keep trying.

Once he drove with Mr Bo down to Parchman to help the guards chase down an escaped prisoner they said was headed toward the Stevens' line last time they saw him running. Another occasion he volunteered to help clean and paint the Methodist Church. But most of the time he stayed on the Stevens' place doing what he was told to do next, thankful to have a next thing to do. God help the person who didn't have a next thing in their life to do, then remembered something from the Bible he'd heard once, something about people without a vision perishing.

He kept his family's cemetery cleaned out, the grass cut back, stabilized the wrought-iron fence where it had come loose in its moorings and re-painted it. He took a bucket of water with Clorox and steel wool and rubbed down the headstones, gave the inscriptions new life. Miss Floy let him cut flowers from the beds around their house, and he arranged them in Mason jars and put them on the graves.

He made his way up to Tutwiler late one Saturday. Billy Bryson's used car lot was easy to find beneath a mammoth sign and triangular pennants of many colors flapping in the wind suggesting a circus come to town. They hadn't seen each other since high school. Billy was glad to see him. They sat on the cinderblock stoop of his makeshift sales shack smoking and talking about old times as if they were much further removed in time. Then he told Billy he'd come to buy a car and they looked at a few. He kicked a few tires like he'd seen his father do once, trying to act like he knew what he was doing. Got in a couple, surveyed their interiors, rubbed his hands over the upholstery, started them up and listened to their engines. He could take them for a drive Billy told him but he declined, afraid he might not stop once he hit the highway. He settled on a '50 Ford sedan, dark blue with shiny hubcaps and fenderskirts. Then Billy told him the price and how he could finance it through the bank, estimated the monthly payments from a little brown book he had. Jo Shelby told him he'd have to think about it, which was a lie because he'd already killed the idea and buried it. With a priceless shooting iron that was almost part of his body in hock in a Mexican pawn-shop, no way he was doing the same with his life to a bank.

He wrote Carmen, wondering why he hadn't already, the way the name kept popping up in his thinking. He asked if she would check on the gun for him, tell the shop owner he was saving up the money, would already have it if he hadn't had his teeth fixed. He wanted to tell her he was thinking of her then decided his life was complicated enough. If he ever told a woman that again, he was going to be sure.

He retrieved his great-grandmother's letters from the trunk where he'd stored them, read them again, slowly, carefully, more attentive this time to what was unsaid than said, any hints or suggestions, secret messages implied between the lines about the land and who might inherit it. Maybe she wrote in code in case the letters fell into Union hands, he conjectured, then reread them all, pouring over them in the evenings, attempting to glean any pattern or design suggestive of hidden meaning. But none was detected.

He wondered again if there had not been other letters and, if so, what happened to them. He'd asked before he went to Mexico and Miss Pat had said that was all of them. But something kept nagging at him, that there might be one or two somewhere, one or two telling Foster what to do with the land and the house, if they had been deeded over to him or not. Or a will. He'd almost forgotten about the will. It didn't have to be anything fancy, lawyer Darden said, just something written in the colonel's own handwriting. Everybody wrote wills. No telling where the old colonel's was. He was too smart to not leave a will.

He answered Senor Garcia's letter, told him where he was and what he was doing, but that he wasn't sure how long he'd be there, then using his Mexican friend's code said his campaign for Governor wasn't going as well as he'd thought it would. He asked of the Senora and her health, of Carmen and her work, her life. He told them of the letter he'd written to her and hoped he would hear from her. He told him about the gun in the Cuernavaca pawn shop, of its value to him, that he had six months to get it back and only two months left, which was another reason he'd written his daughter. When he finished, he reread the four pages, noticing two were about Carmen, and Carmen alone, the images of her playing more and more on his mind.

Sundays he went to church, prayer meetings on Wednesday evenings, always taking along his mother's old Bible she'd left in the trunk. It was frayed around the edges with a loose binding but he handled it carefully and found in its ancient backings much that was helpful. A genealogy at the front where he traced, one more time, his family's lineage. Newspaper clippings, one announcing his parents' marriage and another his grandmother's obituary, several about the church. A couple of recipes. Underlined passages. Scraps of notes lodged between the folds of pages. A memorable one she had apparently written to his father in church—Jo Shelby is outgrowing his Sunday suit. And his father's scribbled response—Ain't he though. One night he went through it cover to cover, page by page, thinking it might give up a deed or a will, or the hint of a deed and a will, something that would help him in his search, but it did not. If the old colonel had had a will, it was not passed down in any Bible this side of the family. It might have been in one passed through the generations in Mexico where Bibles seemed to mean more to folks than they did in America. He still had Senora Moncada's address and would write to her. Maybe they kept wills in places like the Registry. Maybe she would go there for him and find it. If she couldn't, maybe Carmen could, wishing he'd mentioned that in his letter to her. Lawyer Darden said if it was probated there would be a record of it in the courthouse. He needed to see Lawyer Darden, see what he'd found out, tell him why he couldn't sign the paper, of the other plan he'd come up with.

Then came Easter weekend. She'd said she'd be home Easter and surely she would. Easter was like Christmas. Everybody came home for Easter.

After work Friday evening he showered and dressed, put on a white shirt, the gray slacks and navy blue sports coat she'd helped him buy. He walked the few miles down the narrow macadam road to the brick pillars and stood beneath the arch where the wrought-iron letters above him spelled PATRICK, spelled DOMINION.

He waited.

Back and forth between the pillars he paced. It didn't matter that a Patrick might drive through at any time. He was on public property and they couldn't make him go away. The dusk came and went and night set in and still no sign of her, no detection in the distance of the smooth throaty hum of the T-bird approaching, a sound unlike all others that turned the wheels of that world. He sat and smoked a cigarette, thought. About what day it was, Good Friday, that the toughest place a person could be was between Good Friday and Easter, between crucifixion and resurrection. About the disciples and their blasted hopes and how they all ran and only the women stayed. He would be like the women and stay. If she never came ... he'd decide what to do later. He sure as hell wasn't staying where he was forever. But he needed to be sure.

Easter Sunday came but to him it still felt like Good Friday. Dressed up in his best, he went to church with the Stevens and worshipped along with the rest of the community who needed that one day of the year to catch up with their religion. He sat where he usually sat, in his family's pew across from the Patricks, where Athen always sat. Where as children they'd passed drawings across the aisle, then as teenagers, notes. Where he'd expected her to be today. Where her absence loomed larger than an empty tomb and he hoped, still, she might appear. But she never did.

Monday morning he rose early, got up and looked out the window to see if he'd heard what he thought he heard. It wasn't pouring but the rain was falling steady enough if it kept up there'd be no work in the fields, at least not till afternoon, which made him feel better about asking Mr Bo for the morning off and use of the truck. He bathed and dressed and ate a bowl of Corn Flakes and bananas and drank two cups of coffee.

She was standing midway the stairs when he opened the door headed down. She had a serious look on her face and was wearing blue jeans and a sweatshirt with a huge Colonel Rebel on the front, white tennis shoes with no socks. Her hair was disheveled and her eyes had a sad, worried urgency about them. I thought we'd not had enough time to talk, she said.

How come you're not in school? he said.

It's spring holidays. We don't go back until Tuesday.

I thought you'd come home Easter. I wrote you a letter. Called a couple of times.

I'm sorry, Jo Shelby. I went to the coast with some sorority sisters. I never got a letter from you. Nor any messages. It's really been crazy at the house. Miss Lucy, our housemother, usually answers the phone but she's been ill and a lot falls through the cracks when she's out. I apologize.

Neither had moved from where they stood.

Wonder why you didn't get the letter, he said.

How did you address it?

He told her and she told him he had to put Oxford, Mississippi on it.

I figured everybody knew where Ole Miss was, he said, glancing at the symbol of ownership on her sweatshirt.

She smiled. They certainly should, shouldn't they. Can I come up?

You're about there already, he said, returning the smile and waving her up.

There was only one chair in the small room so they sat Indian style on the floor across from each other, their knees almost touching, the way so many of their talks had begun.

Her eyes searched his face. Where to begin, she said. By her downward inflection it was not a question but a sigh, one of frustration.

We can begin with why you left. You left because I'm trying to find out who really owns this land.

It's much more complicated than that, Jo Shelby.

He wanted her to say more but she just sat there looking at him. It was a look that said I love you but am afraid to give my love to you. A look that said I want to be in your world but I'm having trouble escaping the one I'm in. Because I'm a child of the Delta elite, cream of the crop, compacted in that attitude as far down in the layers of skin and flesh and bones as the first flood laid the first blanket of silt over the undefined land. If he could look through that look, he would see that far, what Sissy saw when she said she saw it comin.

Nothing complicated about being friends, he said. We're still friends. You said that in the note you left. Friends talk to one another. You never came back.

Jo Shelby, I intended to. But I couldn't. The house was a war zone. Mama and Daddy were fit to be tied, ranting and raving, calling me up, blessing me out.

About what?

What happened at the Ruleville Club. The entire Delta heard about it. My sorority sisters and friends at Ole Miss had heard about it before I even returned to school.

Didn't know it caused that big of a stir.

I say stir. A tornado would be more like it. There was no way I was coming back and putting me or you through that.

I reckon you told your folks what really happened at the Ruleville Club, that their boys were drunk.

I did.

What'd they say?

Daddy said he was going to have a talk with them.

That's all.

Yes.

Too bad he didn't have that talk a bit sooner.

Why?

He told her what happened to him later that same evening, that he never saw their faces but knew their voices.

She almost came off the floor. Both of her hands flew into the air and came down on his knees. Jo Shelby, that's horrible. Didn't you tell daddy?

Now that'd be one fine hiddy-do. Knock on the door and tell him your sons beat the shit out of me. And I'll bet you a sunrise tomorrow they didn't tell him either.

She let out an exasperated Oh! Well, *I'm* going to tell him.

I'd be much obliged if you didn't. What goes around comes around. That's why I talked Mr Bo out of calling the law. I know they're your brothers and all, but I'll deal with them in due time. What'd your folks say to you?

Of course, they were upset I had a date with you and took you to the Ruleville Club. No big surprise there. She rolled her eyes in mock exasperation. Daddy was more upset than mama. He started laying down the law, as he calls it. Told me if I continued seeing you not to come back home, he'd take my car away, wouldn't pay for my graduate school in Atlanta.

Graduate school?

I'm sorry, Jo Shelby. That's something I haven't told you. I just learned the other day I'd been accepted. I'm going to work on my master's degree at Emory University while I'm teaching in Atlanta.

What else hadn't you told me?

He was going to cut me out of everything, including his will, if I had any more to do with you.

There was a long silence. The rain continued to whisper steadily on the roof, against the windows that rattled now and then with gusts of wind and occasionally they'd hear the roll of distant thunder.

A will's a terrible thing to be cut out of, he finally said.

Her eyes flared. A will's a piece of paper. My life is flesh, blood and bones and a mind that can think for itself. I don't owe my daddy anything and he owes me nothing. Love doesn't owe. Love gives. He can have the car. I'll have a job and can buy my own, pay my own way through graduate school. But none of that is why I didn't call or write you. I meant what I said in the note. We need time to figure ourselves out before we can start trying to solve the problem of us. I'm working on me. I'm not too sure how far along you are working on you.

I'm hittin a pretty good stride. Go on. I can tell you're not through.

I'm not, she continued. I've told you before how I hate this whole way of life down here. I've seen what it's done to my mama and daddy, to my brothers, how it's all they know, like there's a world full of books but they've only read one, keep reading it over and over, same beginning, same ending, same characters, same everything. There's more to life than doing the same thing all the time. I don't want to spend the rest of my life on land that gives nothing back but money and material things. I want a life of my own. That's why I've studied to be a teacher, to do something different rather than coming back to a world of bridge parties and Junior League and debutantes and cotillion and Saturday night dinners at the Ruleville Club. That's why I want to get my master's degree, maybe even my doctorate. Who knows? So when you told me what you wanted to do, it hit me like a revelation straight from heaven. He's just like them. That's all he's interested in, too, the land.

Her words stung. He pushed himself up and stood, feeling the need to be on his feet and not his butt. You got that right. I am interested in the land. But it isn't just the land, he said. Land by itself isn't anything. It's the people living on it that give it life. He stopped and thought, recalling Senora Garcia's words about land and the passion and love people give to it. He walked to a window and looked out, pointed a finger in the direction of his vision. Come to think of it, I don't give a flying shit about the land. He was sorry he'd said shit but she'd made him mad and shit was his mad word, as if that was where his anger stayed most of the time, buried that deep inside of him so when he let it out it was already backed up and primed to let loose and fly. He turned from the window and began pacing.

But I do give a shit about what's right and wrong, he continued, what's due a man and what's not, what's paid off and what's not. I figured. He stopped pacing and bent low so his face was near hers. I figured, he said again, then stopped again.

What did you figure? she said, looking up into his face.

Gimme a second. I'm refiguring.

For a few moments nothing was said as he continued standing over her, his face blank, his thoughts spinning behind his unblinking eyes.

I figured if we got married, I wouldn't have to worry about any deed to the land.

So you were going to marry me for the land, that it?

No'me, and you know it. It was just *part* of my figuring.

But if we married, daddy was going to take me out of his will.

That's where I was refiguring. If I could prove the land still belonged to the Ferguson line, you wouldn't lose anything. We'd both win.

She rolled her eyes. Wrong, she said sharply. I'd still be stuck here in the Delta doing the same ole shit. Since you brought the word up, it seems appropriate.

Same isn't all that bad, he said, trying to recover ground he knew he'd lost. There's somethin to be said for same. It's somethin you can trust. Without same you wouldn't know what to trust. Take the good Lord, for instance. Like the Bible says, He's the same day in and day out, sunrise to sunset. We could go to Mexico. I got a place down there. Family, too. They need teachers down there. It's a beautiful country, mountains and all. Makes this same flat Delta here your talking about look like the dark side of the moon.

She stood facing him, arms akimbo. Jo Shelby, we're talking about two different things, she said, her voice rising. I'm talking about growing and you're talking about a dream, as if this land is some fantasy world, as if getting it back in your family's name has some self-righteous magic about it all, as if the world turns on family name and land. I've got to deal with what's real. And what's real is I've got to get on with my life, have my own family and not be owned by another's. You've got to decide which matters the most, the past or the future. I should have known all this when you took off half-cocked to Mexico, then you opened my eyes when you said what you did that night after the Ruleville Club.

This land don't own me, he said. I don't have to stay here. Might not, in fact.

Her face turned softer as she leaned in toward him, a look of prayerful conviction. Yes, you do, Jo Shelby Ferguson, her words carrying the emphasis a whisper carries. This is where you were raised, where your parents are buried and theirs before them, stretching back a hundred years. That's why you followed those letters to a foreign land and learned what you learned there and why you came back. It's in your blood. We're just two different people caught in the same trap, our families and their histories and traditions, both trying to come into our own.

She stopped. They both stood looking at each other, their eyes steady, unblinking.

That's the most sense you've made since we've been talking, he said. He walked to the window and looked out, her words still echoing.

Never really thought about it like that, both of us up against the same thing, he said, still gazing out the window, at the thing they were up against. She nodded.

He turned around and crossed the room and faced her. Guess what makes us different is you're fightin it your way and I'm fightin it mine. You have to leave to win and I have to stay, for the time being at least. I can't give you all the reasons just yet. But it's not all self-righteous. It's for more than just me and my family. I'll say that. He wasn't sure at this point what he could trust her with, the grandiose plans unfolding in his mind, far beyond anything he had ever imagined, ideas carted back from Mexico that might breathe some new life into other folks' dreams. What she might take back to her mama and daddy, let slip, accidentally or otherwise, the old blood and water difference playing again in his head. A person has to live with their self, he said. Make sure their heart's right, then do what they gotta do. I respect you for that. Hope you can me.

I do, she said, her eyes moist, tears gathering in the corners.

Can't ask for more than that, he said, He pulled her to him and she put her arms around him. He held her tight, pressed his cheek against her hair, whispered her name and she whispered his back, then he dropped his arms and released her.

Don't reckon we changed very much, did we? he said, forcing a weak smile.

I think we did, she said, wiping her eyes, smiling faintly. At least we understand each other now.

Where do we go from here? he said.

I guess we make the choices we have to make, see what happens. I'll finish school in a few weeks, then go to Washington and work in Senator Stennis' office two months, something else that came in the mail the other day, then back here to pack for Atlanta.

So you're goin.

Yes. At this point. And what about you?

He thought a moment. I've been thinking about college.

Ole Miss?

Naw. Delta State. Cleveland's closer. Need to buy me a car first.

She smiled. I like that. She leaned into him on tiptoe and kissed him on the cheek.

When will I see you again?

I won't be home again until school's out, exams and all. Then I go straight to Washington, fly from Memphis. Maybe then.

He watched her cross the room toward the door, squaring her shoulders, holding them erect, as if to show him all she'd said had come from her, something called Athen. She stopped at the door, turned.

I guess growin up together and being best friends for forever isn't enough sometimes, he said. There's too much else in the way.

I guess. But that's not the way I had dreamed it.

Me either.

We are still friends, she said, her lips trembling as she gave a final smile and wave, then he watched her disappear through the door and listened to her footsteps as they faded down the stairs until all he could hear was the birds chirping outside, a signal the rain had stopped.

For a long time he stood there, long after the sound of her car had vanished, wondering what had been gained and what had been lost between them and in the wondering decided it was something that surely couldn't be subtracted. He had to do what he had to do and she did likewise and if they ever did come together every thing would equal. There wouldn't be a remainder.

So, you're back, Mr Darden said as he entered the colorless room, a skylight overhead providing the only illumination. He was wearing a brown seersucker suit with a red-and-silver striped tie, the clash of color and geometry causing Jo Shelby's eyes to blink out of natural sequence.

Yessir. I've made my decision.

You're still aiming to go through with it? Mr Darden said, pulling out a chair and seating himself at the end of the long table across from him. No second thoughts.

Yessir. That is the second thought. Comes a time a person needs to do what's right.

Sometimes right isn't always what's practical, Mr Darden said.

I know. Thought about that, too. If I'd been practical, I'd never found my family, what's left of it. Guess practical's not a part of my nature.

Very well. We just need to formalize all this, sign the contract.

I've thought about that, too. I'd like to change the contract.

Mr Ferguson, I'll declare if you're not just about as confusing as the problem you're trying to solve. Quit beating around the bush, boy.

He winced on the word boy, but let it pass. To the wise and seasoned embodiment of law sitting across from him he was probably acting like one.

I want to be my own lawyer, he said. Want you to help me, kinda like a coach.

Mr Darden leaned back in his chair, his eyes wide, absorbent. Guess I put that notion in your head when I mentioned studying law to you.

No sir. It's just something personal, something I feel I need to do.

Finding Sitting Bull was something personal for Custer, too.

I know that story, read about it in school. But I'm not stupid. I know what happened to my family and can tell it without you having to take notes and retell it, leavin out the most important part.

And that would be?

What's not said.

What's not said?

Yep. I figure I can make a jury *feel* it, he said placing a hand over his heart.

Hold your horses a second, young man. This case, if it ever gets that far, won't be presented before any jury but before a judge, a chancery judge, who's got more power than the governor, more power than a pardon.

I don't understand.

Any and all land litigation has to be tried in chancery court. You've got an uphill battle as it goes, to use the metaphor we've seemed to agree upon. A chancery judge has tremendous power, power that's binding on an appellate court, which is where cases are appealed if they're lost and an appellate court almost never overrides a chancellor. All a chancellor needs is one fact to support his ruling. Doesn't matter if you present him with twenty, if he comes up with one he can hang his hat on, then it's over. Feeling's got nothing to do with it. You've got one big mountain to climb and it's not the enemy waiting for you at the top but an all-powerful judge who needs only one thunderbolt fact to his liking to knock you off. And all of this is going to take place in Sunflower County where the wealthy planters elect the judges and the judges know this like they know breathing keeps them alive so they find facts galore, root for them like a hog, invent them if they can't find them, poof them magically out of thin air, to keep their office. He was raised out of his chair half-standing and half-sitting, his blanched pulpy hands flat on the dark polished table, his eyes leaning, too, in that projected anticipation of something ready to pounce. You get my point?

Yessir. Sounds like somebody made that judge God.

Close to it.

It ain't right.

The world isn't right, Mr Ferguson, he said, raising his voice again and leaning further over the table so his face was nose to nose with Jo Shelby's. It's wrong and right all mixed up together. My job, and yours, too, is to whack away at as much wrong as we can, give what's right more room to grow.

You're not backing out.

No, far from it. I'll help you, he said with a smug gruffness as he eased himself back into his chair, a look of mild irritation on his face. Besides, you'll need someone to examine you when you take the witness stand on your own behalf.

That'd just be one question, he said. Would you tell us the story? I could ask myself that.

The old attorney rolled his eyes. You're still going to need help, Mr Ferguson. Your chances are slim to none at best, but we're breaking new ground with this case. Might even establish a precedent, set a benchmark, go all the way to the Supreme Court. The law is a vicious and ruthless jungle. Who knows. You might be able to get something out of it.

Somethin'd be better than nothin. Reckon not tryin's worse 'n tryin and comin up short.

I wouldn't argue that point with you. He leaned again across the table, his eyes dark and serious beneath the wiry jutted brows, and rapped a bony knuckle on it. Patrick's gotten too big for his britches. Time to take him down a notch or two. Like you said the first day we met, get a leg up.

That's the kind of rithmetic I like, he said grinning.

Mr Darden chuckled. We don't have to change the contract. I'm still your attorney and you're still using my services. I'll be in court if you need me. Having gotten a feel for you I think you'd want it that way, some type of payment of services guaranteed, I mean. Ethical and all.

I just want what's fair.

Good. If you want to pay me more than a quarter's profit from the first year's net earnings, that's your business, he winked teasingly. I'm in this more for the ride than the money. I've made good money. Time to enjoy a little of it. Mary Lou, he hollered over his shoulder. Bring me that Ferguson contract.

Quick steps pitter-pattered down the hallway. Mary Lou entered carrying the contract and quietly laid it on the table between them. Mr Darden reached inside his coat pocket, retrieved a fancy-looking dark pen with gold trim, signed the document and pushed it across the table along with the pen. Jo Shelby signed on the line beneath the attorney's name and pushed it back.

Guess that oughtta do it, he said.

For the contract, at least, Mr Darden said, thanking Mary Lou, who took the document and departed in the same quiet and unassuming manner as she had entered.

I've already done some preliminary work, he continued, opening the manila folder on the table in front of him. I was at the courthouse on another matter. While I was there I checked on the deed to the Patrick property, along with any probated wills and I'll say one thing. You sure knew your history. Foster transferred title to a Quentin Marshall, November 9, 1875. Marshall, in turn, transferred it to a Jack Hurley Patrick, Sr. August 28, 1913 who, when he died on March 21, 1936, willed it to Jack Hurley Patrick, Jr.

That doesn't look good, does it?

It's never looked good. Remember what I told you about adverse possession and statute of limitations, that if Marshall claimed ownership and was on the land for ten years or more, it's his, by law. In other words he had color of title. What makes it look worse for you is that Foster and his descendants were on notice the title had changed hands and did nothing to contest it. They didn't exercise any interest of ownership. The fact Foster stayed on the property, and his descendants after him, does present a problem.

He was just doing what he had to do to feed his family.

I understand, but the fact he stayed on the property means he acquiesced. We talked about that before.

Jo Shelby nodded.

What's in your favor, and will be our major thrust, is that little legal thing called law of descent and distribution. You remember all that, understand it?

Think I do. All we gotta show is that Marshall and old man Patrick knew something was wrong when they made their deal, that there was this cloud hanging over it.

Pretty damn close.

You said you checked on the wills, Jo Shelby said. Find the Colonel's?

No. And I didn't really expect to, not after the history you told me.

How bout the rest of em?

So happens I did, but there's nothing in them. Nothing of any substance, just personal items passed down.

Remember any? He unfolded his hands and leaned back from the table, like a man making room for cards to be dealt.

Mr Darden glanced at the ceiling, massaged his chin meditatively with a thumb and forefinger, struck a finger in the air and looked across at him. I recall a gun Foster willed to his son Nathan. I remember that because it was in every will down to your folks.

Yessir. That gun a Navy Colt?

Come to think of it, believe it was. 45 caliber.

Silence in the small library, the only sounds the sporadic pecking of a typewriter down the hall. Dust motes floated in a column of gray light from the overhead casement and for a moment something else moved in that muted luminance, the mere evocation of the relic, like that of a sacred word sounded, suddenly stirring images blooming upward through the swirling mote-filled beam. Of soldiers galloping through the dust of battle, sabers in one hand and six-shooters in the other, the crack and pop of arms, shouts and yells that defied mimicry, the gray ghosts of another time and his grandfather generations removed among them, rising and falling in his saddle, the gun raised in action, its bronze agleam like something struck from sunlight itself. He sat there in what was the present, the past assailing the thin boundary, then it was gone, the vision as ephemeral as the light on which it rode.

I say something that upset you?

No sir, Jo Shelby said. Just had to think a minute. What day is it?

Saturday, April 16. Why?

Maybe I got time.

Time for what?

It's a long story. Has to do with that gun.

Mr Ferguson, you've got more long stories than folks past a hundred.

I'm hoping they'll get shorter.

You mind letting me in on it.

No sir, he said then told him the story he hadn't told before because it would've used up his hour on the first visit.

I'll declare, Mr Darden said, penduluming his head back and forth in disbelief. If your life isn't one grand epic. And you're still wet behind the ears.

The wet dried up a few years back. What's an epic?

Now that *is* a long story.

You remember anything else in those wills?

There were some letters. It just said letters, C. Ferguson. They were passed down like the gun. There were other items, all personal, but those stand out.

They oughtta. Those letters are the reason I'm here. Cept I don't think I got em all.

How's that?

I spect the Patricks got one or two of em squirreled away somewhere, one or two of em that say somethin bout a will, an unprobated one.

Like I said, if you could find that it might help, especially if it divides the inheritance in equal shares among the remaining children. You don't have to have it to develop your case. It would help strengthen it.

Speaking of which, when's this trial take place? I'm rarin to go, he said, leaning across the table again.

You're going to have to be patient. We're only halfway there. I've got to file a petition in chancery court. It's called an action to quiet and confirm title. Then we have to run a notice in the county newspaper once a week for four weeks, put the entire world on notice, get a summons issued. Then the chancellor sets the date. All that could take a while.

How much of a while?

Months, maybe. With a little luck I may be able to get it on the docket sooner. The judge who'll be hearing the case is new. Biddy's his name. If cases settle and he can clear his docket. You just never know with the law. It's always day to day.

Years to years, sounds more like it.

The old attorney smiled. Sometimes it just depends on how the judge feels. Sometimes there are other cases ahead of us and we have to wait. Biddy does owe me a favor. I might be able to get him to give it a special setting. That would be the only case tried that day.

That's what I want. Don't want this in a crowd.

You may have no choice. You're going up against one of the largest land-holders in the area. We run those notices, it might draw attention.

Won't draw that much attention. All I want is us and the Patricks and the judge.

You'll have a witness or two.

Those, too, then. But that's all.

Very well. I'll contact the judge and get the earliest special setting I can. But it could be a while, maybe even into the fall, September or longer.

Guess I'll just have to wait. I've waited this long.

It was late afternoon when he stepped from the attorney's office onto a sidewalk smoking from the earlier rain. The sun was breaking through the clouds, its sultry heat erasing hopes of a cooler dusk. He stopped at the drug-store on the corner, sat at the counter and ate a tuna sandwich and drank a Coke, all the time thinking what he should do next. He paid his check and was about to leave when a Western Union sign near the pharmacy at the rear of the store caught his eye and he wondered why he hadn't thought of that before. He asked the young girl behind the counter how much it cost to send a telegram to Mexico and she said he'd have to ask the owner and nodded toward the back of the store where a man in a white jacket looked busy filling prescriptions. He thanked her and paid his bill.

Mexico? the man in the white jacket said, flashing a big smile, as though the request were made in jest, not one to be taken seriously. He looked to be about forty, slightly balding with several strands of blonde hair combed downward over his forehead.

Yessir. It's real important.

The man quit smiling and gave him a studied look. Never had anyone send a telegram to Mexico. I'd have to do some figuring.

I got time.

Very well. I've got to fill this prescription then I'll check on it.

He thanked the man and drifted over to the magazine rack beside the front window, began flipping through a dog-eared issue of *Life*, looked at the pictures. He questioned how the store made any money off magazines if a person could look till his heart's content and not buy any, then decided that was what got people into the store. Magazines about life, living and its many angles. The man called out he was ready and Jo Shelby returned the magazine to its rack, walked back to the small counter beneath the Western Union sign.

How long's your telegram going to be? the man said.

Not long.

If it's twenty-two words or under it's only two dollars fifty-three cents. So if you don't get too wordy, it won't cost you much.

I'm not wordy.

The man pushed a pad and pencil across the counter to him. Here, just write out what you want to say then I can figure from there.

Jo Shelby took the pencil, stared at the blank sheet on the pad, his mind as empty. He stood there a long time looking at the pad.

Forgot what you wanted to say? the man said.

No sir. Hadn't forgot. Just don't know how to say it.

Very well, the man said, bringing both hands down on the counter in a gesture of gentle exasperation. If you need me, holler. I'll fill another prescription, and he walked back to the pharmacy section.

Pencil still in hand, Jo Shelby stood and thought. He thought a long time, scratched out a sentence, a second, then another, began counting the words and stopped.

You charge for periods? he called out to the man.

The man chuckled. No sir. Nothing for periods, question marks either, and laughed.

Jo Shelby started over again counting. Forty one.

Damn, he whispered to himself. I must be wordier than I thought.

What's that? the man said.

Nothin. Just talkin to myself. He looked a while at the three sentences, how he could make them shorter.

Be glad to help you, the man said licking a label and slapping it on a bottle.

Jo Shelby looked at him, at the dark yellow-brown lethal-looking phial the pharmacist was holding and wondered why medicines that were supposed to heal were always put into bottles the color of death. He looked back down at the three sentences he'd crafted then back up at the man. All right. Guess you done this before.

Almost every day, the man said, picking up pencil and pad and scrutinizing the three sentences. He laid the pad back on the counter, turning it so it faced Jo Shelby. This is what I'd do, mister ...

Ferguson. Jo Shelby Ferguson.

Pleased to meet you Mr. Ferguson. Carl Whiteside.

You can just call me Jo Shelby, he said shaking the man's extended hand that felt smooth and cool as a woman's.

Very well, Jo Shelby. I'd strike these words in the first sentence, these in the second and these in the third, he said, drawing lines through the words as he went. There. We've cut it about in half.

You mean it doesn't have to be a whole sentence?

No sir. Just so you get the message across.

Why didn't you say so? I don't even think in whole sentences.

You didn't ask.

I'm much obliged. In that case I can go you one better.

Yeah?

Yeah, he said, taking the pencil from Mr Whiteside and quickly striking several more words, leaving GET GUN. WILL SEND MONEY LATER. THANK YOU. JO SHELBY. Then he slashed a line through YOU, added an S to THANK and wrote CARMEN at the top. Got it down to ten, eleven with her name.

Got to have her whole name and address, Mr Whiteside said, leaning over and examining the bare-bones inscription, its evocative mystery. It goes on there, too. You don't want to wire the money with it?

No sir. It's at home.

Where do you live?

Rome. Stevens, place.

Bo Stevens?

Yessir.

Good customer of mine. You work for him?

Yessir.

How much money you need to wire.

A hundred dollars.

Tell you what I'll do. I'll advance you the hundred, put it on Bo's account. You can pay him or come back and pay me in the next couple of days. That way I'm covered.

Jo Shelby thought. The old gunsmith in Cuernavaca had bought it for eighty dollars and agreed to hold it six months for him to buy it back for a hundred. The problem was not the money, which he had, but the time, which he figured was near lapsed. The count between his fingers and head said less than half a month. He didn't want to be in hock to Mr Bo then remembered about his gun collection and what he'd said about the gun. If he were standing there he'd slap the money on the counter in a shake.

That'd be mighty kind, he said, picking up the pencil again and striking through the words WILL SEND MONEY LATER, so the telegram now read GET GUN. THANKS. JO SHELBY.

Unless she's got a long address, you can add more words.

Nope. That about says it.

Good, Mr Whiteside said. Go ahead and print the woman's full name and address. It'll cost more, of course, to wire the money with it.

He nodded his understanding and printed her name in full along with the address he'd memorized:

Carmen Rosario Garcia
13 Avenido Toltecas
Ciudad de Mexico
Mexico

That's in Spanish, Mr Whiteside said, planting an astonished finger beneath the address.

Yep.

So, Jo Shelby Ferguson. You don't think in sentences but you know Spanish.

Guess so.

That's pretty unusual for someone in Sunflower County.

Nobody in Sunflower County's been where I've been.

Where's that? Mr Whiteside said, his finger still anchored to the pad as though stuck there.

That's a long story.

Got to do with this gun? he said, finally moving his finger up the page so it rested beneath the word.

Partly.

Hmmmm. Must be some story.

Yessir. And it's not over.

When's it going to be over?

Directly. Next few weeks maybe. It'll be in the papers.

Don't say?

Do say. How much I owe you?

Mr Whiteside was still looking at him, beholding him like he might some sideshow oddity, some abnormality suddenly plopped down into his tame and normal routine. Oh, that'll be ... let's see. Yanked back from his distraction he began counting the words. Comes to two dollars fifty-three for the telegram then two dollars for wiring the money, grand total of four dollars and fifty-three cents. You could trim it up a bit if you dropped her middle name.

No sir. That'd be like dropping my middle name. Then I'd be just any ole Jo. That woman isn't any ole Carmen. Her mother either. Sorry about that. There I go gettin into that story.

I'd love to hear it.

Don't have time to tell it. Here's your money, he said, pulling out his billfold and tweezering out five one-dollar bills.

Mr Whiteside took the money and walked over to a cash register, punched the keys and pulled the lever. The drawer zinged open and little white tabs that said $4.53 popped up in the narrow window. He slotted the five bills and withdrew some coins and returned to the counter.

Here's your change. I'll get the message out for you this afternoon.

How long'll it take to get there? Jo Shelby said, shoving the loose change into his jeans pocket.

To Mexico City, quick as a flash, he said snapping his fingers. To where that lady lives, depends on how fast they can get it to her.

Jo Shelby groaned.

Something wrong?

No sir. Things just don't move very fast in Mexico, not fast at all.

Can't move much slower than things here.

We're a foot race compared to them.

That so?

Es verdad, then caught himself. Sorry. It's so. Much obliged for your help.

Don't mention it, Jo Shelby. I'll keep a look out in the paper.

He bid the man farewell, turned and headed for the door, surprised at the Spanish popping out like it did, that just sending her a message of so few words would do that.

He was at the door then turned around and returned to the counter.

Forgot something? Mr Whiteside said.

Yessir. You said I could add something and it wouldn't cost me any more.

Yessir. You could add a few more words.

Only need one.

Not a problem, Mr Whiteside said, placing the form once more on the counter before him.

Jo Shelby picked up the pencil and inscribed the word LOVE between THANKS and JO SHELBY.

You can add more, if you want, Mr Whiteside said.

Much obliged, but that one pretty much says it.

He stopped at the door again and walked back to the counter.

Decided to add a few more after all, Mr Whiteside said, and winked.

Nope. Need to take that last one off.

Take it off?

Yep. I'm not there yet. You don't have time to hear that story either.

It was late afternoon by the time he made it back to the highway and began the hike north toward Rome, wondering if he'd done the right thing, asking Carmen to get the gun. She knew how important it was to him and had said she'd help him. He'd left the gunsmith's name and address with her. Cuernavaca wasn't that far from Mexico City. She went there frequently to visit friends, she'd said. All he had to do was write to her, tell her what to do and she'd do it, she'd said. She was his friend, she'd said. She wanted to be more than his friend. She didn't say that, but he sensed it. In the way she looked at him and touched him. The way she spoke to him, that soft accented voice slipping up under his emotions and playing with them, working on them, like she knew all along what she was doing.

He walked a mile before catching a ride with an old Negro man on a tractor. He was headed home, he said, home, of all places, the Patrick plantation. Jake had sent him to Drew to get the tractor fixed, but by the sounds of the miss-firing engine and its uneven rhythm either something else was wrong with it or the old colored man had been taken. He'd catch it from Jake when he got home, the worried look on his old face with the flesh hanging from the bone already telling Jo Shelby that. He was a wiry sight, bent over the wheel as though connected to it, needing it for support, his light frame barely depressing the coiled seat. Tipped at a jaunty angle atop his head was a tattered sweat-stained fedora, its original shape long lost from the half-century vintage it looked to be. When he smiled, Jo Shelby could see he had no upper teeth, just a slick pink ridge of gum gleaming wetly, and only a few lower that protruded from the floor of his mouth at odd twisted angles, like ancient tombstones tormented by time and weather and the shifting of the earth, for his face had that ruined color about it, of land used for only one purpose.

His name was Jefferson, he said, and he'd been on the plantation all his life, born there in fact. There was something familiar about him, though in the time Jo Shelby had lived on the place, he'd didn't recall meeting the man nor the man him and they talked about that, a farm so big two folks' paths never crossed. He did know Jo Shelby's father, however, and spoke highly of Mister John, as he called him, how he was always friendly and understanding, never spoke a harsh word, which he couldn't say about some others he wouldn't mention. Balanced on the wheel fender, his feet anchored on the axle, Jo Shelby thanked him for his kind words and they talked on above the hesitant motor's clacking clamor and the roar of passing traffic. About the land and its crops, the weather, Jefferson's wife, his children, how he had one in college at Rust in Holly Springs and another enrolling that fall at Mississippi Industrial College in the same city. He said the two schools were across the road from one another and didn't understand why they couldn't just be one, that for heaven's sakes, they were both colored and that theme led them into other concerns they pondered philosophically. Thinking it innocent enough and good fodder for talk, and considering they had a number of slow miles to go, Jo Shelby told him why he'd been in Drew, the history of the plantation, of his visit with the attorney, and his case against the Patricks, Jefferson remarking, zat right, zat right, after every statement. Then he told him what he would do with the land if he won the case and the old Negro bounced high in his seat as though suddenly propelled, grabbing for his hat to keep it from flying off, then turned his eyes on Jo Shelby, a pair of large bright black pupils floating on white-engorged balls. You don't say. My woman and me, we'd have our own place?

Yessir.

Well now aint you sumpthin, aint you sumpthin, he said, calming himself, clucking at the tractor as though it might have been a mule, his dream stretching that far back in time.

It'd be yours. You could do anything you wanted with it, but you'd probably keep farming.

Jefferson looked down at the wheel he was holding as though it was suddenly something he recognized and not a habit to which his hands had conformed over the years. His jubilee grew suddenly calm and his face turned somber. I sees, he said. I sees. Cept this here tractor, it belong to mistuh Jake. How I gonna farm without no tractor?

I've thought about that, Mister Jefferson. He reached over and laid a hand on his shoulder. You'll have a tractor and the riggings with it. It'll all be fair and square, like it's s'posed to be in the land of the free.

Praise de Lawd, praise de Lawd. His hands momentarily left the wheel and rose skyward, remaining in that uplifted adulation so long Jo Shelby thought he might need to grab the wheel. An impatient motorist honked from behind then swerved angrily around them, the driver shouting an obscenity as he passed.

They rode the rest of the way in silence, Jefferson bobbing beatifically on the seat, Jo Shelby riding the curvature of the wheel-fender in the warmth of the new friendship, that he'd met someone else who knew his parents, who'd worked the land with his father.

The letter may have arrived that day or several days before, no telling how long it had been at the Patricks'. Maybe weeks. Miss Floy just said Mr Pat had dropped it off that morning she said, handing it to Jo Shelby after Jefferson dropped him off.

It was addressed to him, Senor Jo Shelby Ferguson, Patrick Plantation, Rome, Mississippi. Then at the bottom on the left, in large block letters: PLEASE FORWARD, as if the writer knew they were dealing with a rolling stone. The return address in the upper left hand corner took up the rest of the envelope: Carlita Cruz Moncada, La Hacienda Tierra del Puenta, Estado de Morelos, Jiutepec, LaJoya, Mexico.

How in the hell, he murmured to himself, clutching the envelop in hands still vibrating from the tractor ride with Jefferson. He never told her an address and didn't recall writing one on the note he left behind, so she must have pieced it all together in those brief memorable moments and he marveled at her mind and its years, its sharpness and durability. The envelope was of normal size but felt fragile, the paper very thin, something that had to be opened with care. He was hungry after the long emotional day but would fix himself something to eat later.

He mounted the stairs and retrieved from the bedstand drawer the letter opener he'd carved in prison, worked it into a corner of the envelop and briskly flicked it across the top, the seal slitting evenly along its crease. He looked to make sure the return address, something as precious as the letter, was intact. He knew where she was and could find her again, but doubted his ability to reconstruct her address as well as she had his. Gently, and with great anticipation, he removed the contents, four small white tissue-thin sheets folded once. The handwriting was small and delicate, a reflection of the person attached to the hand, he thought. He glanced first at the date in the upper right hand corner: 17 Marzo, 1955.

Damn, took two months gettin here, he whispered to himself, reflected on that a moment, how long it might have been at the Patricks', then began reading.

Estimado Jo Shelby,

From the kind note you left and all you told me the one night you were here, I know there has been much on your mind and much to accomplish.

So I have been a long time writing on purpose, deliberademente, to allow you time to return to your home in Mississippi, and your novia, perhaps even time to propose and get married, casarse.

The word for marry and home in Spanish are the same, casa. I am sure you know that.

It is my hope the two words come together for you and bring you much happiness.

I must confess I was very sad and disappointed when you left. A bright star had dropped into my otherwise empty heavens, then disappeared as suddenly as it had appeared. There was so much more for us to learn from each other and share. I saw us working together, your helping me with the hacienda. Certainly not restoring it to its greatness—those days are gone forever—but at least keep it from falling further into disrepair. But those were my dreams, not yours. I say that to tell you I understood your reasons for leaving. Everyone has to find their casa in life and perhaps I did help you see where you could find yours.

Now, selfishly, I wish I had remained silent and not been so helpful.

But I cannot be silent now. There is another reason

I am writing to you. After you left, Ricardo quit working for me and made Maria quit as well, so I am in need of an administrador as well as a housekeeper. How silly of him to quit over a gun. He said he was humiliated to return it, that I had robbed him of his honor. Maria was very upset.

She may come back, but I doubt it. They have moved to Jiutepec. You know the situation with my other sons.

Frederico and Raul have no interest in bringing their families here. Their children are in schools that are good for them and there is no school here. Juan is lazy and irresponsible and would not work even if he came. You, Jo Shelby, are the only family I feel I have. So it is to you this old woman appeals.

You said you would return some day to see me, that I could count on that, your words. I do not have much to offer except hard work, a roof over your head, food which I can provide even it I have to cook it myself, and the land itself someday.

No one else wants it and you inquired of it, spoke of it with great feeling, as though it were your own. Something else I must tell you. Government officials are writing constantly telling me they are going to take away the hacienda if I do not pay my taxes and some other monies I do not understand.

There was barely a profit last year, not enough to make these payments they are demanding.

Jo Shelby, I pray for your help. If you cannot come, I will surely understand. I dreamed the other night that maybe you and your novia might come. There is land here for you.

There is a future here for you. If I do not ask, I fear will I not receive and that is the spirit of my request.

Regardless of your decision, please write to me, tell me of your new life, all that is happening with you.

After all, we are the last of our great families. If for no other reason, we must keep in contact.

I pray that God go with you.

Sinceramente,

Carlita Cruz Moncada

His hands were still trembling when he finished. He thought of the room in which she'd written the letter, of the old Spanish desk with the family crest of pure silver where she'd sat, the oriental rugs beneath her feet and paintings of misty trees on the walls, the long history of the place crowding the large room, crowding her, moving her thoughts. The hacienda had been her life, she'd told him, and that was where she would die. She had saved and worked and denied herself for it, she'd told him. She loved it because she loved the people on it, that it was her duty to take care of them because they were her family. She'd done it pretty much alone. She didn't have to tell him that. It was the unspoken part of the story that told the tale. And now she was losing it, couldn't go it alone anymore, which was probably the real reason it took her so long to write. It took her that long to say it. One more reason, he knew for sure they were kin, the last of the long great family.

He sat on the side of the bed and thought. He reread the letter, making sure he missed nothing, his eyes resting longer on what the senora had said about home and marriage. Whoever invented the English language should have studied Spanish first, he thought, then refolded the pages, slipped them back into the delicate envelope and laid it on the edge of the bedstand. Because he knew he'd read it again before going to bed, then again when he woke up, maybe even take it with him to church the next day, read it there, too, in the sanctuary, this gift from the Almighty suddenly fallen like manna from heaven into his life.

He continued sitting, thinking. He needed to write her while his thoughts were fresh, but also to post the letter. If hers took two months reaching him, which was twice the normal time, his would take as long on the return route. A lot could happen in two months. Maybe not in Mexico, but in Sunflower County Mississippi two months was an eye-blink of living. You could be going into a grocery store to buy a Coke and candy bar one minute then standing over a dead man just murdered the next. A woman could say she loved you then not-say it before the moon went from dusk to dawn. A plantation could change hands overnight, with the flick of a wrist. Not a dice roll this time but a judge's signature. It could happen any day because the judge set the time, depending on his mood or politics. Or both.

He opened the small drawer of the bed stand and removed the stationary he'd purchased in town along with a pencil he'd recently sharpened. He pushed the lamp aside to allow more space for writing then pondered what he should say.

The next letter he received several days later was short, three sentences neatly typed. The first notice would be running in the county papers next week, something he'd probably want to know, Mr Darden said. The trial date had been set: Monday, July 25, nine o'clock. He needed to be at his office eight o'clock sharp for the ride to Indianola, then yours truly and his initials L.E.D. That was all.

IV

Through the car window he observed the fixed horizon and green rows of summer cotton flick by, the hypnotic effect of their design telegraphing all in the Delta was neat and orderly then Lester Darden turned off the high-way onto Main Street and Jo Shelby saw the courthouse, its gleaming white columns and clock-faced cupola rising like a temple of old against the cloud-less July sky, and the crowd teeming around it like it was the Fourth.

Sure are lots of folks here, Jo Shelby said.

Mr Darden made no comment as he angled the car into a slot where a staked sign said RESERVED FOR ATTORNEYS.

They got out of the car and entered the double gate of the iron fence that encircled the grounds. The sun was raining heat and the hour not yet nine o'clock.

Like I said, sure are lots of folks.

Mr Darden made no reply, his eyes straight ahead as he walked slow and steady, swinging his bulging leather briefcase as though it propelled him along.

Don't suppose those notices you ran were headlines, he said.

Nope, Mr Darden said. But they might as well've been. Word gets around whenever there's a deed challenge to a landholder, especially one whose name happens to be Jack Hurley Patrick. I thought I had prepared you for that.

Yeah, but these folks don't look like they could walk up and lay a nickel on the counter in the dime store. You'd think it was election day.

Might, Mr Darden said. Cept for all the nigras, a tone of question in his voice. They were near the steps, the words no sooner spoken and Jo Shelby looked up and saw Jefferson leaning on one of the massive columns smoking a cigarette, others of his race from the Patrick place gathered around him. He glanced right and there was Sissy, standing at the opposite end of the porch. She had on a white dress he'd never seen her wear and white low-heeled shoes her feet bulged in, as though that was why her brow was pushed down and her eyes were hooded. A sudden wild thought spun in a splinter of light bounced off a chrome bumper in the distance, then struck him like a revelation. Several days before he'd stopped by her house for a visit. She'd made a comment to him about the trial: Sho is nice what you gonna try and do for us, she'd said, her eyes on the land across the road as she rocked. He asked how she knew and she said Jefferson had told her. What she didn't tell him, that simple logic quickly falling into place as he looked around him, was that Jefferson had told everyone of his kind on the place, stretching the story a little here and there, so that this Monday morning the Patrick plantation was probably at a stand-still, brought to its knees by the high blood and the low back, the high sugar and down in the mouth and swole feet, all those complaints and excuses his father had heard over and over for not working, now piled up on the steps of the county courthouse hoping for some relief, some hope of ownership of land neither they nor their kin before them had ever had. And he, Jo Shelby Ferguson, suddenly the savior who'd bring it to them. Holy shit, he murmured.

What's that? Mr Darden said as they mounted the granite block steps spooned smooth by half a century's comings and goings.

Nothin. You were right. Word does get around.

Inside the courthouse people lined the long wide halls. They gathered around office doorways and loitered around the lone Coke machine and sat on the iron steps to the courtroom a story above, all awaiting a signal from the bailiff the courtroom was open. By their coveralls and brogans and two-toned foreheads, most of the men were tenant farmers and sharecroppers from out in the county. A few had on white shirts and ties, a sign they were of the town, bankers or lawyers or store clerks. The women wore summer print dresses. A few had on heels. Some of the Negroes were dressed in the plain black and white suits and dresses and shoes they'd worn to church the day before. The rest wore what they'd worked in the past week, and would the week ahead, years to come, as well, that being one decision poor folks didn't have to make. What they'd put on when they got up each day.

The courtroom was empty when they entered, the cavernous hall echoing their entrance. Mr Darden walked on ahead of him, but Jo Shelby stopped, giving his eyes, his memory, a moment to adjust. Bolts of sunlight, strong and distinct as trusses shoring up the walls, shot through the tall windows and dust stirred by the ceiling fans high overhead swirled in the bright angled beams like flakes of gold trapped in a liquid tube and it was all too familiar to him.

I wanted us to come early, Mr Darden said, let you get used to the courtroom.

Don't reckon I could get more used to this one.

That's right. I keep forgetting.

I hadn't stopped, he said, boring his eyes into the table where he sat the longest week of his life.

He followed the attorney through the swinging gate of the bar, its dull whomp whomp sound behind them in the still air reminding him when it once seemed the door to his life, everything hinging on the witnesses passing through it.

This'll be us here, Mr Darden said, setting his briefcase on one of the two tables facing the judge's bench.

Jo Shelby stopped, a grim look on his face. I'd be much obliged if we used the other one.

That's the respondent's table. You're the complainant, the one contesting.

They look the same to me. A table's a table.

I understand, Jo Shelby, but from his honor's viewpoint, Mr Darden said, pointing toward the bench, there is a big difference. Point number one about trying cases. Don't piss the judge off. And sure as hell don't piss him off before you open your mouth.

Jo Shelby laid his knapsack on the table. He pulled out a chair, scruti-
nized it a while, the wear along its arms, configurations of worn varnish and
finish he had memorized, given names like he would to clouds on summer
days when he had nothing else to do. He pushed the chair back under the
table. Think I'll just walk around a bit. I can think better standin up.

That's good. Because you'll be standing a lot.

From a door behind the judge's bench a young woman came carrying
note pads and pencils and began setting up her station to the right of the
judge's bench. An older lady followed. She had gray hair piled on her head
like a beehive and strutted with an air of authority. She carried an armful of
file folders, one of which she carefully placed on the judge's bench and the
rest on a table immediately beneath. Next she'd fill the water pitchers on the
attorneys' tables and the bench and put clean cafe-looking glasses beside
them. Then the aged bailiff would come out wearing his brown uniform,
pants sagging from his waist beneath the weight of a wide belt loaded with
bullets and a pistol he not only had never fired but probably couldn't because he didn't know the trigger from the safety. He'd walk over to the
windows and adjust the blinds so the sun wouldn't shine directly in the
judge's eyes, then walk back and sit in his chair to make sure then walk
through the courtroom adjusting all the chairs so they were just where he
wanted them. Mr Darden had explained to him it was chancery and not cir-
cuit court, that they were different courts, with different people. But Jo
Shelby bet it ran the same anyway. Because there were rituals set down thou-
sands of years ago that made the law what it was. That made him sit in the
same chair at the same table again.

You might want to take a little time and look over your notes, Mr
Darden said, settling himself comfortably into a chair. The bailiff had not
yet entered and the court reporter and the older lady had left so it was just
the two of them again in the courtroom.

Don't have any, he said from the jury box where he'd been leaning on
the railing, temporarily lost in thought, lost in the memory of why he went
to prison. Why twelve men in that same rectangular enclosure found him
guilty when he was innocent as the pure driven snow. Why God let his parents get killed while he was in and why he went to Mexico when he got out

and found what he was looking for only to turn around and come back in the same night, not even giving the moon time to set or sun time enough to rise again. Why the wherewithals and notwithstandings and whys and what ifs of his life had come down to this moment and what he was going to do with it.

Mr Darden rose half-way in his chair, You don't have any? then lowered himself, as if the rising had been necessary to draw attention to the question.

Yep. He walked toward the table where MrDarden was seated. Don't need em.

Good God, Jo Shelby, his voice boomed in the chambered quiet. This time he stood up, rapped both knuckles on the desk. This is the most complex, intricate, convoluted case I've ever let myself get involved in. I've got an entire briefcase of notes and case law covering everything from A to Z. And my associate, who is not even a lawyer, tells me he doesn't need any notes.

A B C's far as I'm going. What's convoluted mean?

Coiled. Twisted.

Jo Shelby placed his knuckles on the table and leaned across so the two were counterpoised in a shaft of light penetrating the old shadowy chamber. We're gonna untwist it, he said, his eyes steady, unblinking on those of the old attorney across from him.

You know something, Jo Shelby, Mr Darden said, his face as set, as serious. For a moment there I thought I saw a flash of revenge in your eyes.

Jo Shelby blinked but didn't move.

You hear what I said? Mr Darden said.

I heard it.

I'm not talking about a hundred-year-old revenge, but something more recent in time.

Jo Shelby said nothing, kept staring into his attorney's eyes, his thoughts spinning on the words suddenly turned on him.

I'm not talking about—

I know. You're not talking bout justice but getting even.

Jo Shelby, you have to take emotion out of this. If you've got no notes, you've got no map. If you've got no map, your thoughts are liable to go anywhere, like a runaway river. Just remember. When you stand in front of that judge and present your case, he doesn't give a damn what happened to you seven years ago, or whenever it was. But you sure as hell have got to make him care what happened eighty years ago, then again forty-two years ago when the Patricks acquired this land.

Jo Shelby nodded, stood erect then walked around the table and took a seat beside Mr Darden. You got a pencil and some paper?

Mr Darden leaned over the arm of his chair, opened his briefcase and handed him a long yellow pad and a pencil. If you wear that one down, I've got more, he said, pointing at the pencil and winking.

Jo Shelby propped the pad on a raised knee and licked the tip of the pencil. He was about to write when he heard a commotion in the back of the courtroom and quickly turned around. He knew they'd be there. Sooner or later, he knew he'd see them. But sometimes knowing is not knowing, a vague foreboding of the real thing, and his eyes were still not prepared for the spectacle he saw bursting through the courtroom doors.

Carrying a black briefcase a tall gangly man led the way. He was wearing a blue pinstripe suit and two-color shoes and strutted with an air of ownership, as if to say I've been here many times and this is my territory. Close behind him were Mr and Miss Pat and Jake and Josh and their wives then slamming against his eyes, Athen in a bright red dress and black heels.

He'd gotten one letter from her since he'd last seen her, on stationary bearing the official seal of Senator John C. Stennis. The only flight she could get from Memphis to Washington left the evening of the day of her final exam. She'd gotten an extension on her internship and would be back mid-August, it said. She was thinking about him and would see him when she got back, it said. It didn't say she'd see him in court. It didn't say anything about the case, which she had to have known about, had pumped and drilled into her by her mama and daddy and two brothers and all of them now lined up on the other side like a blood bank and he sat there wondering what happened to the cocky spirit that said nobody owned her.

Mr and Miss Pat and the tall man in the well-pressed suit, their lawyer Jo Shelby surmised, took their seats at the other table across the room to his right while the rest in the party sat behind them across the bar on the first row. Jo Shelby kept looking at Athen, studying her. We have to make our own choices and see what happens, she'd said the last time they were together. He'd made his and from where she was sitting now, he guessed she'd made hers, the next thing to happen a foregone conclusion. He hoped she'd look his way, but she did not. She glanced at the ceiling, at the big fans turning slowly. She looked out the window. She toyed with her purse and adjusted her skirt around her legs, which stirred memories, how they'd felt locking around him, driving him into her that night. His heart sank.

Are you all right? Mr Darden leaned over and whispered.

Yessir, he said, and he turned around and began writing.

The older lady with the beehive hairdo came back out carrying a tray of glasses and pitchers filled with iced water, put them in their appropriate places then departed with the same ceremonious prissiness as she had entered. The bailiff came out and sat in the judge's chair, swiveled it around to face the eastern windows and Jo Shelby saw it was, indeed, the same deputy who'd been on duty during his trial. His hair looked whiter and longer, the length by design, perhaps, as if it added a little more of the court to him, a little more authority. He continued watching the old-man-playing-cowboy, for he had that child-like air of make-believe about him as he pushed himself from the throne-like chair, strutted over and lowered the blinds according to his estimation, then began arranging the chairs behind the gated area to their predetermined positions, his movements deliberate and precise. The lady with the beehive hairdo came out and took her seat, then the court reporter. Everyone waited in silence.

She's not the chancery clerk, Jo Shelby whispered, nodding at the older woman. Where's he?

She's the deputy clerk, Mr Darden whispered back. Don't know where Doom is. But we'll see, and he winked.

At the first dong of the belfry clock the bailiff opened the doors and allowed the spectators in. A heavy rumbling overhead caused everyone to turn and look at the balcony filling up, black faces peering down. Jo Shelby spotted Sissy on the front row and Jefferson behind her and past that he could see only the tops of heads, wall to wall and all the way back. He turned back around. The balcony's full of colored folks, he leaned over to Mr Darden and whispered.

Believe it is, Mr Darden whispered back, distracted, his next comment as though he might not have heard him. Never seen anything like it. Been practicing law over fifty years and never seen as much interest in a chancery matter. You got any general idea why all those nigras are sitting up there?

Jo Shelby nodded, cupped his hand around his mouth and whispered back. Got a gen'ral idea.

Mind letting your co-counsel in on it?

He told him what he'd planned to do with the land if he won it back, about his conversation with Jefferson, and Sissy's remark, how word had apparently gotten around the plantation.

He needn't go any further, Mr Darden interrupted him loudly, his eyes wide, brows riding his forehead to his hairline. Why didn't you tell me this? he said, modulating his voice back to a whisper.

Didn't think it was important.

Important, hell. You could start a damn revolution.

I thought that was the gen'ral idea, Jo Shelby said, grinning.

Mr Darden rolled his eyes and dropped the pencil he'd been holding. Good Lord, man. The Delta's already loaded up to blow sky high. Wouldn't take much. Besides that, the land's not yours to give away. We went over all that. This is about the descendants in Mexico, the ones who own three-fourths, who never got the word. You sure you don't want me handling this?

Their muted conversation was drawing attention from the other table.

I'm sure. What I'm not so sure bout is that lawyer feller over there. He's been givin me the evil eye. Looks mean as a snake.

Mr Darden leaned in again. Snake doesn't come close. Try alligator.

Jo Shelby gave him a serious look.

Now, you sure you don't want me to handle this for you? Mr Darden said. I won't charge you any extra.

Yep. I'm sure. I'm not afraid of alligators. What's his name?

Minski.

Sounds foreign. Where's he from?

The name's Polish but he's from Mississippi. Tupelo.

All rise, the bailiff said in a loud voice. He was standing erect as a soldier at attention beside a door behind the bench.

The judge entered with a flourish and took his seat. He was a tall, slender man, in his fifties, Jo Shelby guessed, with thinning black hair, large ears and a small mouth. He didn't look like a judge but more like a preacher, or Sunday school teacher, not anyone that had been bought or could be bought even if he did owe Mr Darden a favor. The judge swiveled the chair toward the windows and regarded them, as if checking to make sure the bailiff had done his job correctly, then swiveled back and opened the manila folder in front of him and spoke:

The matter before the court today is case number 6666, Jo Shelby Ferguson et al versus Jack Hurley Patrick et al. What says the complainant?

Jo Shelby leaned into Mr Darden. Who's et al? I thought it was just me and him.

It means others, your kin in Mexico and Jack Hurley's, too, Mr Darden whispered back, then stood and directed his attention to the judge. The complainant is ready your honor. If it please the court, Mr Ferguson will be serving *pro se* with my assistance.

Very well, Mr Darden. You'd mentioned that before to me and the court accepts him in that capacity. What says the respondent?

The respondent is ready, your honor, Mr Minski said, pushing himself up, half-rising from his chair.

Are there any motions, any other matters to take before the court, the judge said.

No sir, Mr Darden and Mr Minski said loudly in unison.

Then the complainants may call their first witness, the judge said.

Mr Darden wrote something on his legal pad and shoved it in front of Jo Shelby, then nudged him. Jo Shelby looked at the two words scrawled on the pad and stood, a slight tremor in his knees, in his fingertips as they steadied him against the table. Mr Darden had rehearsed him, what to say and how to say it, when to say it. The only thing Jo Shelby hadn't done was say it live in front of a crowd he hadn't expected. In front of them. Of her. Now that the moment had arrived his jaws were locked back to his ears and his tongue frozen to the roof of his mouth, the heat rising and sweat running and he wished he had more of a map than he had. He took a deep breath then the first words came:

If it please the court. He paused. He knew that much. He just needed to keep talking and the rest would come. Because the history was all right there in his head, packed in behind his voice and all he had to do was start it and it'd play itself, like a record spinning on a phonograph. He looked down at the legal pad, at the two words written on it.

Your honor, I call Mr Jack Hurley Patrick. He glanced at the pad again and the two words. Adverse witness, he said. I'm callin him as a adverse witness. Mr Darden had told him that if he called Mr Pat first as an adverse witness, he'd get another crack at him later, two shots instead of one, an economy he needed because the other side was loaded for bear.

Jack Hurley Patrick will take the stand, the judge said.

The big man strode forward, raised his large right hand before the deputy clerk, placed the other on the Bible and repeated the oath that he would tell the truth, the whole truth and nothing but the truth so help him God.

Jo Shelby had always wondered why all that had to be said. All they needed to do was swear to tell the truth. The truth was the truth, no halves or fourths about it. It was either the truth or it wasn't. And if you swore you were going to tell the truth, that said it all. You didn't have to ask for God's help to tell the truth. That was already understood because God didn't truck with anything but the truth. He looked over and watched Athen watching it happen. He watched the other attorney who was still giving him the evil eye and that was the spark that fired him. He'd been hurt by Athen. He'd been hurt by Mr Pat. Hurt by Josh and Jake. Hurt by the system. Hurt by the loss of his mama and daddy and granddaddy. Hurt by people in Mexico he never saw and never knew. Hurt in places he didn't even know he could hurt. But God help the son of a bitch who didn't even know him and tried to hurt him because he was paid to do it. That was the fire he needed.

Tell us your name, please sir, he said to Mr Pat, feeling foolish as he said it. Mr Darden had said he'd have to, along with a lot of other things he'd have to say that made no sense. But that was the law, Mr Darden had said, and likened it to the rules of a game, that without them there would be no game. Because there'd be no boundaries and no one would ever win or lose.

Jack Hurley Patrick, his deep voice boomed from the witness stand. He sat hunched over, his hands folded before him, his eyes narrowed and riveted on Jo Shelby.

Mr Pat. I mean, Mr Patrick. Mr Darden had told him everything had to be kept formal. Even if he put Athen on the stand, which he wouldn't, he had to address her as Miss Patrick. Mr Patrick, he continued, I know where you live, but I've been told—he turned and glanced at Mr Darden—I have to ask you anyhow.

I live on the Patrick plantation in Rome, Mississippi, he said, an icy edge in his voice.

Yessir, I know. But it has an address, doesn't it?

Mr Pat looked perturbed and screwed his nose around. That's all I know. That's how we get our mail. He said it with that air to his voice, that arrogance of place, of the planter class not needing an address because the whole world knew them that well.

How about route one, box one? That sound about right to you?

Mr Pat heaved his bulk erect in his chair. Guess that's right.

Mr Darden slid a piece of paper across the table to Jo Shelby and he picked it up. And this right here shows all the land you claim to own.

Mr Darden rose from his chair. Your honor, let the record show Mr Ferguson is referring to the deed to the Patrick property and we wish to enter that into evidence at this time. He nodded for Jo Shelby to take the document to the court reporter to be stamped, which he did then returned to the table. He looked down at the notes he'd hastily put together then back up at Mr Pat.

There's a graveyard on your place, isn't it?

Objection, Mr Minski shouted, springing to his feet. Leading question.

Overruled, the judge said. Mr Minski, you've been in this court many times. Surely you know leading questions may be asked of an adverse witness, then lowered his eyes on Jo Shelby—Mr Ferguson, you can ask leading questions of this witness, but no others, unless they're adverse witnesses as well.

Yessir, thank you, your honor.

Very well. Let's proceed. The witness can answer the question.

I forgot what the question was, judge, Mr Pat said.

Have you got a graveyard, a cemetery on your place? Jo Shelby said.

Yes.

Is where it's at now the place it's always been?

Mr Pat thought again. No sir. Don't think so.

Where was it first?

It was in the peach orchard, behind the house.

Where is it now?

Out in a cotton field.

You know how it got there, Mr. Patrick?

I do.

How'd it get there?

My daddy moved it.

Why'd he move it?

Cause it was a cemetery and it was too close to the house.

Cause it was somebody else's cemetery.

You making a statement or asking me a question, Mr Pat said.

Minski half rose in his chair, then sat back down.

I'm askin, Jo Shelby said. Didn't he move it cause it wasn't his family's, but somebody else's?

I don't know. I didn't ask him.

Jo Shelby paused. New sweat followed old down his face and body and he could hear the cardboard funeral fans beating the air behind him. He glanced across at Athen, who was looking hard at him, then down at the legal pad in front of him. All right. It got moved, he continued. Where'd it get moved to?

He had the graves dug up and the caskets moved further back into the trees, Mr Pat said. I remember him telling me it took five niggers—he glanced up at the balcony—five negras and two teams of mules a week to do it. He tried to leave it as nat'ral as he could, put all the markers back into place, the wrought-iron fence just like it was.

You said that was in the trees?

Yes. That's what I said. Blood was up in his cheeks and his head was twisting a little from side to side, like a man needing to loosen his collar and pull his tie down a notch.

Where is it now? Jo Shelby pressed.

Same place.

But it doesn't look the same. Why's that?

Cause we needed more acreage and cleared the trees. Mr. Patrick said. We left the cemetery where it was. Didn't bother a thing. Even left the trees in it.

It's out there now and you plow around it just like you been doin to my family all these years.

Minski rose again, opened his mouth to shout another objection then sat down, as if the getting up and down was becoming too much trouble and he didn't want to piss the judge off but the judge was already getting ruffled.

Mr Ferguson, just stick to your questions, the judge said.

Yessir. I forgot. Seems like a lot's been forgot.

That's for the court to decide, the judge said, irritation cracking in his voice. Don't make your own editorial comments. Just stay with your questions.

All right. And who's buried in it?

Mr Pat sat there silent a few seconds looking puzzled then answered the question. Like you said, your family's buried there.

Jo Shelby stopped a moment, flipped a page on the pad. How'd you come by that property, the one that's described in the deed?

Got it from my daddy. Inherited it.

How'd he git it?

Believe he bought it from a feller named Marshall, back in nineteen hundred and thirteen.

Yessir. And how'd that feller Marshall come by the land?

I don't rightly know. That was a long time ago, Mr Pat said looking again at his attorney.

Mr Patrick, you raised your hand and swore you'd tell the truth.

Mr Pat nodded.

Did your daddy ever tell you any secrets about that land?

Secrets? I don't understand.

He ever tell you there was a cloud on that title, that it might not be his out right to leave you?

Mr Minski stood up again. Your honor, I'm going to have to object to this continued line of questioning. This young fellow, out of an abundance of ignorance, I'm sure, continues to assail the procedures of this honored court.

Mr Minski, the judge said, the irritation rising in his voice, first of all, this honored court can take care of itself. Secondly, Mr Ferguson is not out of line, but you're about to be. I will note your continuing objection, but we need to move this along.

Minski slumped down into his seat, his chin on his chest.

Mr Patrick, Mr Ferguson asked if you were aware of any problems with the title, the judge said.

No sir, he said, looking up at the judge.

Mr Darden stood. Your honor, for the record, we have evidence suggesting there was not clear title when the property was first delivered to Mr Marshall in 1875, which the courthouse records will indicate was when title was transferred. That's all Mr Ferguson—

I read your brief, Mr Darden, and am aware of all that, the judge said. Mr Ferguson may continue with his examination of the witness.

Jo Shelby looked at Mr Darden, then down at his pad. Do I do it now? he leaned over and whispered.

Yes, Mr Darden whispered back. Go ahead. He's stonewalling. You're not going to get much else out of him.

Mr Patrick, sir, you ever talk to the chancery clerk about this property?

The witness blinked and twitched his head to one side, as though something unexpected had just flown into the side of it. He thought awhile again, rubbed a hand up and down his thigh. Yep, believe I have.

What'd y'all talk about?

Another long silence, Mr Pat staring now at his attorney with a stupid look on his face, as if he knew an answer but wasn't sure if it was the right one, as if his attorney might magically telegraph it to him. For the life of me, I just don't remember.

Jo Shelby looked over at Minski who was smiling approval. Miss Pat one chair over smiling, too. Athen looked worried. Jo Shelby swung his eyes back on his witness. Your daddy ever talk to the chancery clerk about this property?

I wouldn't know. He never talked to me about his poli ... . He never talked to me about the financial matters.

Financial matters wasn't what I asked you about. You just about said something else. You just about said politics, didn't you?

Well ... no ... I wasn't. I ... uh ... was actually ... you know ... it was his ... policies. I never discussed his policies with him.

This was the trap Mr Darden had told him they would set and Jo Shelby figured it was set about as good as he could set it. Your honor, I don't have any more questions.

Not of this witness at this time, Mr Darden rose and said. But we reserve the right to cross-examine later.

Very well, the judge said. It's in the record. The respondent may cross-examine.

No questions, your honor, Mr Minski said curtly.

The complainants may call their next witness.

Mr Darden was still standing. Your honor, plaintiff co-counsel calls Mr Jo Shelby Ferguson.

Jo Shelby grabbed his knapsack and moved slowly around the same table where he'd sat a half-dozen years before, toward the same chair where he'd proclaimed his innocence and no one heard him because the people who could have come to his defense were the same ones sitting across from him now, and for the same reasons stayed away then. Family name and honor, all wrapped up in the land because they all fed off each other. He turned his head and looked at Athen as he passed through the swinging gate and saw the brow furrowed and dark brown eyes softening, looking at him like they would when he'd fall and she'd come running up to him and say *you all right?* Or they'd be playing and his mother would call and tell him it was time to come in and she'd whine *you gotta go now?* The same that looked at him the time he told her goodbye and left for Mexico. It was more like that time, the one that said goodbye.

He placed his left hand on the Bible, the same as before when he swore he'd tell the truth, and did. He raised his right hand and repeated the same oath and it was as though his life was repeating itself, like an echo taking a long time to get back to him. And for a moment—just a moment—he wasn't even sure where he was in time. Until he mounted the single step and took his seat in the chair and saw her again directly in his line of vision, which snapped him back like an elastic band that's stretched too far.

Mr Ferguson, Mr Darden began, then paused and stepped around the table so he was standing in the open area before the bench. He folded his arms. Would you just tell this court why you're here today. I believe that would be the best way to do this.

Except for the flurry of cardboard fans and muted traffic outside, the courtroom was quiet. Jo Shelby cleared his throat, gripped the knapsack on his lap tighter in his hands, and began. He told the same history he'd told a hundred times, it seemed, only this time it didn't seem like history. He told the story of his family as far back as Calvin Ferguson in Scotland then moved it forward, generation by generation, progeny by progeny, family by family. With no notes before him he cited names and places and dates, connecting them all together in a steady progression of the evolution of his family in America. He opened the knapsack and retrieved the two ancient letters he'd taken with him to Mexico. The frail pages vibrating in his hands, he read them to the court and spoke of others in his possession and retold that journey of a people long ago, then of his own more recent to that country and the discovery there of his lost kin. Reaching again in his knapsack, he pulled out official documents he said were from the Registro in Cuernevaca, Mexico, the government office where family records were kept. Beginning with Carolina Suzanna Ferguson, daughter of Caroline Bouchillan Ferguson, citing birthdates and marriage dates, he traced the family lineage through the generations down to Carlita Navarro Cruz, one of the last of Ferguson descendants on the Mexican side of the family tree and told of his visit with her and of her indomitable and courageous spirit. He told of his visit to the church cemetery where the woman who wrote the letters, his great-great-great grandmother and her husband, the Colonel in question, were buried, slowing down at that point so no one would miss the one card he'd gone to such great lengths to play. But Mr Darden interrupted him before he could get there, making sure, too, no one missed it.

Jo Shelby, tell the court the location of this church.

A little town called La Joya.

And this church, what type of church is it?

It's a Catholic church. They must've become Catholics.

Why is that?

Cause only Catholics can be buried in a Catholic graveyard, or so the people there told me.

Describe for the court where the cemetery is in relation to the church.

Jo Shelby sensed his attorney's intentional slowing of the pace, drawing out of the drama. Not just to get to the one hide-hanging nail he'd drive with a single bang into the tough skin of the law but getting it told with such detail it couldn't be something just made up. It's right behind the church, he said, which is just off the main street that runs through the town. There's not much there. A restaurant and a gas station. A bar or two. The church isn't big but it's got a tower with a bell in it. Like I said the cemetery's right behind it. It's not big, either.

And what did it say on your great grandfather's, on Colonel Ferguson's tombstone? Mr Darden said, taking a step toward him.

Jo Shelby pulled back the flap of the knapsack one more time and pulled out a spiral notebook.

Jo Shelby, Mr Darden said. Would you please tell the court what you're holding in your hand?

It's a little notebook I bought in Mexico.

And why did you buy it?

So I could write down everything. So I could remember it.

Did you write down what was on your great-great-great-grandfather's tombstone?

Yessir.

Would you read it for the court, please?

Un Americano de honor y valor, Jo Shelby said.

In English this time.

An American of honor and courage.

What else was on the tombstone?

Some dates.

And what were they?

When he was born ... and when he died.

When was he born?

March 9, 1805.

Mr Darden turned and walked back to the table then turned again, this time facing the judge. And what was the date of his death, the date you saw there with your own eyes on that tombstone, one that is still there today in that cemetery in La Joya, Mexico for anyone else who wants to go and see?

April 2, 1882.

There was silence in the courtroom. Jo Shelby sat unmoving, watching as Minski hastily wrote something on a pad. As Mr and Miss Pat sat boring holes in him with narrowed eyes. As Athen sat staring at him, a surprised, disbelieving look. Not at what he said, but that he'd actually said it. And he wasn't through.

Mr Darden walked back to the table, picked up a piece of paper and faced the judge. Your honor, let the record show that the recorded date of Colonel Calvin T. Ferguson's death, April 2, 1882, is seven years after the date on a copy of the deed I hold in my hand, the same that has been offered into evidence regarding said property. Complainants also move to place into evidence the two letters from Jo Shelby Ferguson's great-great-great grandmother, Caroline Bouchillan Ferguson, along with the genealogical documents from the Registro in Cuernavaca, Mexico and his notebook.

Minski shot up again, a finger in the air. We object, your honor, he shouted. All of this is gross and flagrant, manufactured hearsay.

I'm going to let it into the record, the judge said. I'll decide later how much weight to give it.

Jo Shelby remembered what Mr Darden had said about a chancery judge needing only one peg to hang his hat on. He hoped he was giving him an entire rack. That way if only one notch survived, that would be enough.

Your honor, may I approach the witness and look at the documents first? Minski said.

You may, the judge said.

Legal pad in hand, Minski walked over to Jo Shelby and Jo Shelby handed him first the letters. Be careful with em, he said. They're real old.

Minski flashed an indignant glare at him then commenced scanning the fragile pages. He made some notes, handed the letters back to Jo Shelby and asked for the genealogical documents. He looked over those, scribbled more notes. He looked at the notebook but wrote nothing, handed it back to Jo Shelby and returned to his seat.

Your honor, again for the record, Minski said, these letters do, indeed, look to be old. But there is not one whit of evidence to support the witness's contention they were written by the individual he is claiming to have written them. The genealogical documents from Mexico, though they bear an official seal, may be bogus. Anyone can obtain official documents in Mexico for a price. The corruptness of the country is common knowledge.

Not as corrupt as some folks I know, Jo Shelby bristled.

The judge banged his gavel. Mr Ferguson you are out of order. You cannot make personal statements from the witness stand.

Sorry, your honor.

Thank you, your honor, Minski said. Furthermore, for the record, the notebook is nothing but rank hearsay.

Again, Mr Minski, your objections are noted, the judge said then looked down at Jo Shelby. Mr Ferguson, I know those items are very valuable to you, but you need to give them to the court reporter for identification. The court will return them to you later.

Jo Shelby handed the items to the court reporter who marked them and set them aside on her small table.

Mr Darden, you may continue with your witness, the judge said.

I have no further questions, your honor.

Respondent may cross-examine, the judge said.

Jo Shelby sat watching the flurry of discussion huddled at the table across from him. Jake and Josh were involved in it, but Athen kept her seat. Then Athen got up and stuck her head into the knotted group and he tried to remember what he'd told her and what she might've passed on. But he hadn't said anything to her he hadn't said today. He'd done the best he could, he told himself. He'd told the truth and it was the truth that set you free the Bible said and there wasn't anyway to unravel that hard fact of God no matter what questions came at him now or who was asking them. He was still sweating rivers but they were cooling rivers now and the shakes were gone from his hands. He looked up into the balcony at the gallery of dark faces, at the different shades, something he'd never noticed, how they were not all one color but different colors and deemed that was why he'd heard them called colored all his life. He wondered how they felt looking down at nothing but white folks that all looked alike and he thought it might be nice, having your own color that set you apart. Then he thought again that they didn't quite see it that way. They were upstairs and not downstairs because the white folks sitting downstairs only saw one color. Their own. Which wasn't even a color but the absence of color. That's what the bobbing heads and whispering mouths at the table in front of him were really all about. Trying to keep the color of ownership from changing. And it couldn't go on forever, not in Mexico, not in America. The truth he'd told might set more than just himself free. That was the hope he saw in the quiet and waiting faces above him in the balcony.

Finally the discussion broke up and everyone sat down.

The respondents have no questions, your honor, Minski rose and said.

Mr Ferguson, you may step down, the judge said.

Jo Shelby walked back to his table and sat down, leaned over to Mr Darden. How come they didn't ask me any questions?

They're going to ask the judge for a directed verdict.

What's that?

It means they don't believe we proved our case and they're going to ask the judge to rule for them.

That doesn't sound good.

Maybe. But I don't think he'll grant it. Excuse me, Mr Darden said and stood up. The complainant rests, your honor.

After he said there'd be a fifteen minute recess, the judge tapped his gavel and there was a rumble of feet and voices as people scurried to line up at one of the few bathrooms or catch a quick smoke.

He remembered the recesses, when everybody else was allowed to get up and move around but he had to stay in his seat, his hands cuffed, feet

shackled and chained, waiting till noon or five o'clock while his bladder
burned like a fire spreading across his thighs and into his stomach, his penis
a knife turned inward. Then they led him out and back to his cell where the
burn exploded through his body until it was no longer burn but the absence
of burn, relief long since a word that had lost its meaning.

Now was not much different. There were no handcuffs or chains and
shackles but he sat there frozen in his seat not knowing what to do. He
didn't need to use the bathroom and didn't want to get up and walk around
in the halls, afraid of who he might bump into, have to talk to, what he
would say if he did. Mr Darden had gone back to the judge's chambers to
discuss an unrelated matter with him. The court reporter and clerk had vacated their stations, and the bailiff was gone, too. He looked around and saw
Athen had left with her parents and brothers. The courtroom was almost
empty. He decided he'd best stay put.

Mr Darden re-entered and returned to his seat and shortly afterward the
courtroom filled once again, everyone in place. The bailiff said, All rise again,
and everyone stood up again and the judge entered with the same flair as
before, as if it was an obligatory act, one his status required. True to Mr
Darden's prediction, Minski rose and requested a directed verdict, presented his argument, rehashing all he'd said before about lack of evidence,
hearsay and statute of limitation, then added something new at the end:

Your honor, the parties' presence here today has nothing to do with this
land and the title to this land but smacks with all the earmarks of unrequited
love. The plaintiff, Mr Ferguson—he pointed at Jo Shelby—is doing nothing but seeking revenge because of his rejection by the daughter of Mr Jack
Hurley Patrick, Athen, who is present here today and prepared to so testify
to that fact.

Jo Shelby jumped up.

His attorney jumped up with him and pushed him back into his seat.
Mr Darden leaned over and whispered in his ear. Don't you dare say a word.
This is just smoke and mirrors. Stay calm.

That's a damn lie. She didn't reject me.

We know that, but don't play into their hands.

Mr Darden then presented his objection to a directed verdict. He recapitulated the history, mentioned all the various pieces of evidence placed before the court, cited several cases. The judge listened patiently, then rendered his decision. The case would continue to its conclusion.

The rest of the day went quickly, and predictably. Minski put Mr Patrick back on the witness stand, then Miss Pat. Josh and Jake followed after lunch. Mid-afternoon there was a lull and it seemed everything that could've been said had been. Then Minski called Athen.

It was a sorrowful look Jo Shelby caught when she glanced at him as she passed through the swinging gate held open for her by the bailiff, a look almost apologetic. Words of his father rose from his memory: *Son, folks in the Delta're loyal to only one thing, the land, more so than even their own families and don't you ever forget it.* And he watched as that high-heeled loyalty hammered her presence into the wooden floor she crossed to stand before the clerk and take her oath, her hand not even in the air when Mr Darden rose.

Your honor, we object to the use of this witness for the purpose counsel has already indicated. This case is about the law and facts related to the law, not about emotion. I fail to see how this witness could add anything new to what has already been said. Whatsoever might have transpired between my client and Miss Patrick is immaterial and irrelevant, intended only to embarrass my client, and furthermore an epitome of the very revenge they falsely claim is being perpetrated on them.

Hands straight at her side, Athen stood stock still before the clerk whose head was turned back toward the judge.

The judge's face was drawn downward and clouded with obvious irritation. The court tends to agree with Mr Darden, Mr Minski, the judge said. I'm not going to allow my court to become a battleground of old love grievances. What further information can this witness add to your case?

Your honor, Mr Minski began, the respondent contends there is no evidence whatsoever indicating a cloud on the title to the property in question. Therefore, the only purpose for our being here today, spending the taxpayers' money—he half-turned and passed an arm over the crowded room, then faced the bench again—is that of retribution. My use of this witness goes to that issue, Mr Ferguson's sole motivation for bringing this suit. I only have one or two questions for her, your honor. I won't be long.

The judge thought a while. What says the complainant?

We continue our objection, your honor. But if the court allows the witness to testify, we may have more than one or two questions on cross.

The judge thought again, longer. A murmur rose from the crowd. Athen continued standing before the clerk, the two facing each other like soldiers at attention, awaiting orders. Forewarned by his attorney about the power of the Delta planter, Jo Shelby watched the judge, then watched the Patricks watching the judge, wondering what secret contributions might have passed under the table, what tit for tat deal made in one of those restaurants, a fraternity of the landed, in one of those curtained back rooms reserved for the rich. Then he looked at Athen and had to believe she was standing there not of her own will but that of others, because she had been ordered, threatened. His mind swept back over the years of their youth, recalled those times of camaraderie and play, their own private conspiracies against the rules that governed them. Then swept forward to the night beside the lake and he had to believe deep down she still cared for him, would not hurt him. There was too much accumulated between them over the years to be wiped out in a single fight. Because love and care and affection couldn't be cancelled out that easily or quickly. He prayed quietly it would be so but before he could finish his prayer the judge spoke.

I'm going to let the witness testify, Mr Minski. But be brief.

Yes, your honor, Minski said and walked around the table and approached Athen, making a calculated stop, it seemed, blocking Jo Shelby's view of her from where he sat. He scooted back his chair for a better angle and Minski, aware of the movement, took a step backward blocking his vision again.

Please state your name, Minski said.

Athen Patrick.

They don't even want me to look at her Jo Shelby leaned over and said to Mr Darden.

They don't want her looking at you, he said back.

I want her looking at me.

Move to the chair by me, then. You can see her from there and the judge won't let him get any closer to the witness.

And where do you reside, Miss Patrick?

Jo Shelby slipped from his chair and moved quietly to the other side of his attorney and took the empty chair at the end of the table, where he had clear vision of her.

The Patrick plantation, Rome, Mississippi, except when I'm in school at Ole Miss.

Minski took a couple of steps forward.

Mr Minski, the judge said sternly. You know the protocol. You may not approach the witness.

Yessir, your honor, he said and retraced his steps. And you've lived there all your life?

Isn't that a leadin question, Jo Shelby whispered to Mr Darden?

Mr Darden nodded and put a finger to his mouth.

And you've known the plaintiff, Jo Shelby Ferguson—he turned and pointed at him—how long?

All my life. She'd been looking down, not even at the attorney facing her, but with those words she raised her head and looked at Jo Shelby. Not a glance, but a look, one that held and lingered a few seconds.

And is it not a fact, Miss Patrick, that you and Mr Ferguson have been, shall we say, seeing each other, dating, for the past year or so?

She hesitated a moment, moved her hair back with her hand. We've been friends all our lives. And, yes, we've been dating, were dating, for a short time after he came back from Mexico.

Yes, we've all heard about his Mexico trip. And in this time you were dating, is it not a fact he told you he intended to take your father's land away from him because he held him responsible for his incarceration at the state penitentiary at Parchman?

That damn sure is leadin, Jo Shelby leaned over again and said, loud enough to be heard by the entire courtroom.

The judge's gavel came down. Mr Ferguson, I must remind you to remain silent. You or your attorney will get a chance to cross-examine.

Jo Shelby cowered and slumped back into his chair.

The judge then looked at Mr Darden as if anticipating an objection and when none was forthcoming said, you may answer the question, Miss Patrick.

No sir, that is not true, she said, her voice firm, ringing, almost angry.

Minski's head flinched and he rocked backward on his heels. Oh? he said. He paced back and forth in front of his table, in front of the Patricks who looked as stunned. He reached over and picked up a glass of water, took a sip, set it back onto the table.

Maybe I asked you too much, he continued. What did he tell you on that Saturday night of March 19, following an incident at the Ruleville Club, which we need not go into?

Jo Shelby glanced over at Josh and Jake who were smiling at each other, then wrote something hurriedly on his legal pad and shoved it across the table under his attorney's eyes: The hell we don't.

Mr Darden acknowledged the message, as if annoyed by the brief distraction, and continued listening.

He told me all he wanted to do was what was fair, she said, that he owed it to his family.

Minski had the look of a man shot in the back before falling forward.

Jo Shelby sat transfixed. All of a sudden nothing made sense, but everything made sense. She was saying the exact opposite of everything he'd expected, yet everything he'd hoped against hope she would say, like two sentences written over each other, two thoughts that can't stand in the same place, but do.

If it please the court, Minski said and strode back to his table. He leaned over and conferred with Mr and Miss Pat whose confused faces were swinging back and forth in unison. It was a long conference. Josh and Jake got up and stuck their heads into it. Then they sat down and Minski turned around. No further questions, your honor.

Plaintiff may cross-examine, the judge said.

Mr Darden rose. No questions, your honor.

Yessir we do, your honor, sir, Jo Shelby said popping up and quickly maneuvering around his attorney, too quick for the ovaled speechless face to call him back or the marble-veined outstretched hand grab and catch him. Too quick for any stirring from the crowd.

I got a couple, your honor, he said as he stepped behind the podium that had yet to be used. He gripped its worn polished edges to steady himself then looked up into Athen's surprised face, one trapped suddenly between wonder and admiration, one that didn't know which to choose.

Athen. I mean, Miss Patrick, ma'am, would you please tell the court what happened that night at the Ruleville Club?

Athen began unscrolling the events of the evening, describing in detail, as if she might have been an artist sketching a scene, where they sat in the restaurant and who was around them, her brothers' sudden intrusion, what they said. When she told of their ties being tacked to the table the courtroom erupted in a roar of laughter that even brought an incongruous smile to the judge's face as he banged away with his gavel trying to restore order. The Patricks ducked their heads in shaken dismay and Jake and Josh slunk into their coats.

Now, Miss Patrick. His heart was beating like a runaway piston and sweat was pouring from his hands onto the podium. Would you please tell the court what else happened that night?

She fidgeted in the chair a moment, looked at her brothers on the front row, their faces still crimson from the previous embarrassment, then back at Jo Shelby with that same mixed confusion of wonder and admiration.

Yes. I think I can.

Objection, Minski jumped up and shouted. That would be hearsay, your honor.

You don't even know what she's going to say, Mr Minski, the judge said. The witness may proceed.

You told me that—

Objection, you honor, Minski shouted again. For the obvious hearsay reason now.

The judge lowered his head; thought a moment, then looked out over the courtroom, through the windows then back at the crowded courtroom. This is, indeed, a new and unusual situation, he said, addressing no one in particular. The court is fully aware of what hearsay evidence is and what it is not. Statements of a party are not hearsay. Mr Ferguson is here to deny it if it's not true. I'm going to go ahead and let her answer the question. You may have the same latitude on re-direct, Mr Minski.

Minski scowled and sat down.

Jo Shelby recalled what Mr Darden had told him about the power of a chancery judge and how, in all likelihood, it would play against him. But in that fine and fitting moment, he relished its righteous nod in his favor.

The witness may proceed, the judge said.

There was stillness in the courtroom as she told of Jo Shelby's abduction as he had related it to her. Stillness until she told of the blindfold and croker sack over his head and his hands and feet tied and his body tossed from the bed of a pickup onto the hard Delta ground in the dark of night then a chorus of low moans broke the air from the balcony, a funereal hum not unlike the mourning of the dead at a wake then the stillness returned. He stood there a while looking at Athen and she at him, the courtroom silent as church at prayers. He couldn't tell where the knocking was coming from, whether it was his knees or his heart or his teeth, but there was one more question he had to get out before he collapsed.

Miss Patrick. He stalled, looked down at the blank podium, at the pools of his own perspiration, at his own blood, it seemed, drained from white-knuckled hands holding on for dear life, drained from his very heart. Miss Patrick, you put your hand on the Bible and swore to tell the truth and I just got one more question.

She nodded.

Do you still … ? He stopped. His body shook. He raised a trembling hand into the air, held it there as if to signal a pause, that he would finish the question, then he brought it down. I got no more questions, your honor, and he sat down.

Re-direct? the judge said.

Sullen and morose, Minski half-rose from his chair. Nothing further, your honor, his slumped posture betraying his own inner confusion and lack of direction from that point.

Jo Shelby wasn't sure, either, what had happened. Only that her testimony hadn't hurt him and might have helped him. The issue of the land and its deed seemed long forgotten, but there was one final card to play.

The witness may step down, the judge said and Athen made her way back to her seat, through the swinging gate the bailiff held for her, where she paused and looked again at Jo Shelby, one that said *I tried*.

Your honor, the respondents rest, Minski said.

What says the complainant? the judge said.

Your honor, the complainant would conclude with a rebuttal witness. If it please the court, we would call Mr Roy Doom, Chancery Clerk of Sunflower County.

The bailiff left the courtroom to find the clerk who was not immediately available.

Mr Darden crooked his finger at Jo Shelby motioning him to come closer. He's been trying to dodge the subpoena, he whispered to his client. But the deputy caught him across the street after lunch and gave it to him.

Where is he now?

Don't know. But he'll be in contempt of court if he doesn't show.

The bailiff entered through the door behind the judge's bench, followed by the tall old man with the gimp leg and the elevated shoesole, the limp more exaggerated than when Jo Shelby first saw it, he noted, as the gangling chancery clerk hobbled in front of his own deputy clerk and swore to tell the truth, then hobbled up the single step and lowered himself uncomfortably into the straight-back chair.

Mr Darden picked up his legal pad and strode to the podium. Please state your name for the record.

Roy Doom.

And Mr Doom, you've been the chancery clerk of Sunflower County how long?

Forty-three years. Since 1912.

I believe that's just about a record, isn't it, Mr Doom?

I'd say so. Don't plan to quit any time soon, either.

In fact, you've only had opposition four out of your eleven terms and had to make a second primary race only once, in 1919 when you had four opponents. That not right?

Yessir, Doom beamed.

And one of the reasons you've been chancery clerk so long is that you've campaigned vigorously. In fact, it's my understanding, you'd begin in January, ride the train to Rome, some forty odd miles from here, and walk back along the railroad tracks, stopping at all the little stores and towns along the way. And after you did that you rode horseback throughout the county and didn't start using an automobile until sometime in the twenties.

Doom's head bobbed proudly up and down.

That you slept wherever dark caught you and wherever you could find the necessary hospitality and that you were, furthermore, able to call the name of every voter in the county at one time, a list that's now about ten thousand names.

That's an absolute fact, Mr Doom said, the wide gummy smile creasing his face, revealing what was left of his teeth.

This was called softening up the witness, Mr Darden had explained to Jo Shelby, setting him up with a few soft left jabs before landing a hard knockout right.

All this means, then, that you were the chancery clerk in nineteen hundred and thirteen, doesn't it? Doom's head began bobbing up and down and around like the question was words he was trying to dodge and Jo Shelby was hoping Mr Darden would go ahead and land the knockout punch on the old codger, spring the trap shut they'd set.

Yessir.

May I approach the witness, your honor?

The judge nodded.

Mr Darden crossed to the court reporter and picked up a document, handed it to the witness, then stepped back.

So you would have been the chancery clerk when one Dewitt Marshall, on March twenty-one of that year, delivered the deed to Jack Hurley Patrick, Sr., the document you now hold. Is that not so?

Yessir. That would have to be so, Mr Doom said, carefully scrutinizing the piece of paper.

Did Mr Patrick senior ever speak with you about this title, say anything one way or the other about it?

Mr Doom was silent. He sat there with his head still bobbing around, the bobbing becoming about as exaggerated as the limp. Then the head quit bobbing a second for him to reach up and scratch it, the scratching more than was necessary, too, Jo Shelby thought. Then the scratching stopped. Seems like maybe we did, he said.

Now, Mr *DOOM*, Mr Darden said, suddenly pronouncing the name like a gong resonating. With a memory impeccable as yours, able to call any of ten thousand names on the county's current voter rolls, call that person by name on sight, it would seem you would remember a conversation with Mr Patrick senior, especially since it *possibly* had to do with a cloud on this title.

Objection, Minski shouted, immediately on his feet.

I said, possibly, your honor, Mr Darden turned quickly to the judge and said.

Objection overruled, the judge said.

I remind you you're under oath, Mr *DOOM*, the name piercing the air again with such force the tower clock itself might have tolled.

Mr Doom scratched his head some more. Seems we did have a few words about it.

Those few words are why we're here today, Mr Doom. What were they?

Jo Shelby moved to the edge of his seat. Mr Darden was no longer punching softly but hitting hard on the man's memory, like he'd been hammering his name over and over, as though it was some bell of reckoning that would ring in the truth if gonged enough, shake it loose from the old man's rafters where he'd tucked it away and was now about to drop into the lap of the court.

For the life of me, I just don't recollect what they were.

Perhaps I can jog your memory a bit. Did any of those words have to do with one Calvin T. Ferguson, whose name was on the original deed?

Just not sure.

Maybe Foster Ferguson?

Doom shook his head.

Mr Doom, as the chancery clerk, did you not see fit to check the sectional index to see if you were indexing that property in the right place before sanctioning its transference to Mr Patrick senior?

Well, I don't rightly remember. I guess I thought it was aw right. I was told it was aw right.

Who told you it was all right?

Doom's head stopped bobbing. His face looked confused, dazed, as though the jabs coming from Lester Darden had so shaken up his thinking the truth was indeed primed and ready to pop out from the sheer force of needing relief. Mr Patrick, he told me.

No further questions, your honor.

Mr Darden headed back to the table but Jo Shelby was already up meeting him halfway, whispering something frantically in his ear.

Sorry, your honor, Mr Darden said. I do have a couple of more questions.

Mr Doom, do you recognize my client, the plaintiff, Mr Jo Shelby Ferguson? Have you ever seen him before?

Doom looked over at Jo Shelby, squinted his eyes. Might have.

Mr Doom, he's twenty-five years old, voting age, on your voting rolls, one of those ten thousand names you said you had memorized.

Doom's eyes flashed wide open. Yessir. Yessir. That truly is Jo Shelby Ferguson.

Fine. Now, Mr Doom, March fourteenth of this year, a Monday morning, do you recall a discussion with Mr Ferguson in your office?

Doom looked shaken. His face paled. His lips quivered.

Mr Doom, I can call your assistant, Mrs Shaw, to refresh your memory if need be. She introduced Mr Ferguson to you, I believe.

Doom's upper body was now shaking. He seemed stricken, unable to speak.

Yes, Mr Doom? You have an answer? Mr Darden said, his body bowed toward the witness.

Y-y-yes s-s-sir. I think I did ... I mean ... y-y-es ... I d-did speak with the young man.

And what did he tell you?

Mr Doom stuttered and stumbled through the dialogue as best he could remember.

When Mr Ferguson left your office that day, did you then go and place a phone call to Mr Jack Hurley Patrick, Jr sitting right over there, Mr Darden said, pointing at the planter. Remember, Mr Doom, you are under oath.

The only sounds in the courtroom were the rattling of the deed Mr Doom still held in his hand and the near drum roll rhythm of his chair tattooing the small platform. Jo Shelby sat amazed at the wisdom of his attorney. This was a question he'd wanted him to ask Mr Patrick but Mr Darden said if he did, they could confer and work a conspiratorial response, which was why they didn't take their second shot at the planter.

Doom finally pushed out a response to the question. Y-y-y-yes-sir I b-b-believe I did.

And what did you say to him?

I j-just told him what th-th-the boy said.

And why did you do that?

I d-d-dunno. Just th-thought I should.

No further questions, your honor, Mr Darden said and sat down.

Minski rose. Mr Doom, I have only one question. Is that a valid deed you're still holding in your hand?

The paper was still shaking in Doom's hand. Yessir, tis.

Thank you, your honor. No further questions.

The final arguments seemed needless and unnecessary to Jo Shelby, just a repeat of everything that had already been said. Mr Darden stood and began by quoting some scripture and stating that a man's land was a most sacred possession and that taking it from him was a terrible thing, the most heinous of thefts. He hit his strongest points. That the old colonel was still alive when the land was gambled away and thus not Foster's to give in the first place. That a gambling debt was not an enforceable debt, not enforceable by law. That by law, since the colonel had no will or none was available, his children, by descent and distribution would own three-fourths, which meant the descendants in Mexico, and that DeWitt Marshall would only own a fourth. That because there was knowledge of fraud or deceit, or implied knowledge of fraud or deceit, in the transferral of the deed from Marshall to the first Patrick, there was thus a cloud on the title, which by demonstration in the courtroom Mr Doom must have known, and that said descendants had a legitimate claim to the title, at least the challenge of a claim, which was the same in Jo Shelby's mind as putting the Patricks on notice. And that that was the way it was and should be, Mr Darden said, with an air of foregone conclusion, as if to say that was the way it should have been in the first place and all of this was unnecessary.

Minski countered, going on and on about statute of limitations and adverse possession. That the Patricks had paid the taxes all those years. The Fergusons had acquiesced by staying on the land. No knowledge of fraud or deceit had been factually or categorically proven. The papers Jo Shelby presented from the supposed Registro in Mexico were not notarized and could have been easily fabricated. The descendants supposedly living in Mexico were just that, phantom families manufactured in the wild imagination of one vengeful and rejected Jo Shelby Ferguson in a mad grab for restitution. Minski concluded, with an emotional flair and appeal, that what had been done over the years could not be undone, that there was no law in God's Book or under His heaven that would render that right and just. That to take a man's land from him, land that had been cleared by the sweat of the brow and the strain of muscle, by the grinding of bone on bone and the wasting of the flesh, land that had been worked and tended and protected over the years, was a greater theft than the one imagined, concocted, machinated, yea, fictionalized in the imagination of the heartbroken and rejected and otherwise dejected and vengeful. That the law was the law and upon that law of the great and sovereign state of Mississippi and Constitution of the United States of America he rested his case and sat down.

The courtroom was still as a field after a battle and the last shot fired. The judge sat implacable behind his bench and stared at the ceiling as though his decision hovered there, feathered by the whirling fans. Then he spoke. The court is impressed with the arguments of the two distinguished attorneys, he began. This is an unusual case, with unusual circumstances, varying twists and turns, one certainly not to be treated or ruled upon in haste. Therefore, I am taking this matter under advisement.

What's that mean? Jo Shelby leaned over and whispered to Mr Darden.

It means, he glanced up at that balcony, he's not going to start a riot or a revolution by ruling now, Mr Darden whispered back.

Court adjourned, the judge said, bringing the gavel down in a final clap.

The sun spread a bronze light over the land as they drove north on state highway 49, away from the hubbub that had followed the final gavel when a flurry of hands reached across the railing to shake his and swarm him with praise and well-wishes and the hallelujah shouts from the gallery above sounding like a revival celebration and in the midst of it all he'd tried to keep Athen in his sights and make a path to her but it was impossible. He and Mr Darden were swept away with the crowd through the vestibule where Sissy and Jefferson and the other Negroes from the plantation were spilling down the balcony stairs to get to him, hugging and slapping his back and telling him how proud they were, how thankful.

That was quite a reception you got back there, Mr Darden said.

Yeah. Guess it was.

And you deserved it. Even though you scared the everliving shit out of me a time or two, you did one fine job. I'll tell you again, you oughtta study law.

Jo Shelby looked at him and smiled. Maybe I will some day. Right now I'm wondering what the law's gonna say. What do you think?

Don't know, Mr Darden said, his eyes narrowing on the road, as if he hoped to glimpse an answer in the flat and hazy mind-numbing sameness. Judge Biddy fooled me today.

How so?

Well, like I told you, he's newly elected. One of the powers that got him elected was sitting at a table across from him, and I don't mean me or you. I expected him to be much firmer with us, not give us as much leeway. Damn if he didn't even flirt with reversible error a couple of times. May have even committed one, in our favor.

What's reversible error?

That's when the judge makes a mistake and the other side appeals and the appeals court overrules his error.

That means they have to do it all over again.

Sometimes.

Damn. Then it's not in our favor. Nothin's in our favor if we have to go through that all over again. I'd just as soon walk to Egypt.

Nothing more was said for a while as the car wheels whined over the highway and the wind thrashed through the windows.

What if the judge didn't make a mistake? Jo Shelby said. You said he was more powerful than the gov'ner, almost like God, that whatever he said went.

Well, let me ask you this, Jo Shelby. If the judge rules against you, do you want to appeal his ruling, take it to the state Supreme Court, maybe all the way to the United States Supreme Court. It also means a lot of work and expenses.

I don't' know, Jo Shelby said pensively. Guess that's one bridge I can't think about crossin till I get to it.

They drove on.

But I'd still like to know what he might say, Jo Shelby interrupted the quiet of the car.

Your guess as good as mine. Quite frankly, I didn't think you had a chance. Now I'm not so sure. I didn't expect our good chancery clerk to spout off like he did, completely discombobulate and come undone. That certainly laid a basis for deceit, at least implied deceit. We'll just have to see. Regardless of his decision, what do you plan to do?

Jo Shelby watched the rows of cotton flow by in linear progression, their lines straight as strings to the horizon. Don't know. That's the same bridge. By the way, how come you told Mr Doom I was on the voting rolls, when I'm not?

Bluffing. I knew you got your rights back when they released you. Didn't know if you'd re-registered. Figured Doom didn't know either.

Mr Darden drove him back to the Stevens' and let him out in the drive-way, told him he'd make contact as soon as he heard something. Jo Shelby shut the car door, leaned back in the window and thanked him again.

Just one final question, Jo Shelby.

Yessir.

Mind letting your co-counsel in on that question you started with Athen and never finished.

Just somethin personal. I decided the answer didn't matter. That it might embarrass me.

Very well. I think I understand.

I do believe, Mr Darden, sir, whatever happens, we put em on notice. We got a leg up.

We did that, son. We sure nough did that, and he drove off.

The single word lingered in his thoughts, all the way to his apartment, and further still, while he cooked his supper and lay in bed and tried to sleep. *Son.* He couldn't remember how long it had been since he'd heard that and when he closed his eyes the lids squeezed out the tears that had gathered. And they didn't stop for a long time.

It was Saturday afternoon, the sun bright, a cool wind blowing in across the land. He was in the fields atop a tractor spreading chemical poison to kill boll weevils when he saw the car and the plume of dust behind it coming toward him. Then the car stopped on the crop road not far from him and the dust overtook the car. Mr Darden got out, gave a big wave.

It had been over a month since court and he'd begun to wonder if the judge was as all-powerful as he'd been trumped up to be, anybody close to God having to take that long to make up their mind. He'd lost himself in work, that exercise that gobbles up time, arising at five in the morning and working for Mr Bo past six, sometimes seven in the evening, the summer sun yielding more light. Mr Bo told him he didn't have to work that long, but he wanted to make the extra money he told him, that he was saving up. Mr Bo asked him why and said wasn't sure, might need it for college, the same answer he gave Mr Carter who opened a savings account for him at the

Merchants and Farmers Bank. So when he saw his attorney walking toward him he was more than just a sight for sore eyes. He was the bearer of his future.

He clambered down from the tractor and began tromping across the rows toward the lawyer who was wearing the same suit and tie he wore the day he first met him.

Hope you didn't drive all the way out here just to say howdy, Jo Shelby said to him, wiping his hands on a rag looped through his belt.

Nope, Mr Darden said, a big smile on his face.

Hope you don't have that look on your face cause the sun's shinin in it.

Nope, Mr Darden said again, still smiling, and handed him some papers.

What's that?

The judge's decision. We got it this morning. I had Mary Lou make an extra copy for you.

With trembling hands Jo Shelby received the papers, unfolded them and began reading. It took him a while. The language was difficult to understand, all lawyer talk. When he finished, he read the three pages again. Not sure what to make of it, he said. Seems like all I got was the graveyard.

You did, all right, and access to it, Mr Darden said. But read the last two paragraphs.

I already read em, twice.

Read em again.

He pulled out the last page and read the final paragraphs again. It says something about more evidence needed, he said, that we didn't have enough evidence.

That's right.

So that means we lost.

No sir. You won.

I won? Hot damn. Hotdamnamighty, he yelled, raised his eyes to the sky and let out a whoop. Hotdamnamighty.

Hold on, Jo Shelby, Mr Darden said. Don't go celebrating just yet. You won round one. The judge awarded you the cemetery out right, but the rest is yours conditional upon a will or other supporting evidence being located. It says in those two paragraphs that the judge ruled a material fact was possibly concealed when the deed changed hands. He found that ownership was taken with the knowledge, or possible knowledge, of a defect in the title. In other words, he was convinced by your story, the details, but primarily by that inscription on the old Colonel's tombstone.

That was the one peg he hung his hat on, then, Jo Shelby said.

That and the other small ones along with it, including one the respondents contributed.

How's that?

Doom's testimony, which helped establish that a material fact had, in all likelihood, been concealed. Judge Biddy even says as much in his decision, which means the cloud on the title is not entirely dispelled.

So where does all this leave us? You said it was just round one.

Because of a possible missing deed or will or other evidence that might affect everyone's claim, the judge continued the case, left it open sixty days for an additional hearing.

That doesn't sound good. Don't know what I could come up with in sixty days besides what I got.

Mr Darden smiled. Thanks to Minski outsmarting himself, you've got more than sixty days.

How come?

He either didn't read the order carefully or Patrick was putting pressure on him or both. Anyway, he filed an interlocutory appeal which divests the lower court of jurisdiction.

What's interloc ... whatever mean?

To speak in the middle.

That son of a bitch sure did enough of that.

In other words, there'll be no hearing, which means you've got plenty of time to gather additional evidence. In other words, Jo Shelby, he said, thumping him on the shoulder with his finger, you've laid a good legal basis and come out on top to this point. Now all you've got to worry about is finding that will. If you find that will, that should do it.

His face fell. You said that was like looking for a needle in a haystack.

I did. And it is. But you seem to have a particular knack, maybe I should say persistence, at doing that.

How long I got?

The statute of limitations on fraud doesn't start running until the fraud is discovered, which means technically you've got ten years. More realistically, you've got a year and a half to two years, which is how long the ruling on the appeal will take. Because if they win the appeal, it is almost like starting over again for you.

In other words, I need to knock em out in round two.

That's right. Knock them out with a copy of that will. If you found that, that would be the icing on the cake. It wouldn't hurt to have some concrete proof of the time of the colonel's death.

Guess that means goin back to Mexico and gettin a picture of that tombstone, too.

Getting those papers notarized might also help, Mr Darden said.

Then he lowered his eyes and looked at Mr Darden. Don't know if I'm up for all that.

You give it some thought.

I will, he said. I'll have some time to think. One other thing. You said that judge was prob'ly owned by em.

Maybe a new day's dawning, Mr Darden said.

Maybe so. Don't know what to say.

Don't need to say a thing. Just keep in touch. You're an impressive young man with a lot of spunk. And spunk can take a man far in this world. What do you plan to do?

Don't know right away. I got a job here. Been saving up. Might take a look at college, then law school. I'm much obliged to you.

If I can help you in any way, just let me know, Mr Darden said.

They shook hands and the attorney headed back to his car.

Wait a minute, Jo Shelby called after him. I owe you somethin, the contract.

Mr Darden stopped and turned around. You don't owe me a thing, son. I've had the most fun I've had in years. Just seeing Jack Hurley Patrick, Jr. squirm and wiggle nervous as a whore in church was enough payment for me, he said with a grand smile. He started the engine and drove off, that word again settling comfortably into Jo Shelby's thoughts, that he could be a son in every way to someone and not be blood kin.

Monday morning he gave Mr Bo his notice, that Wednesday would be his last day, apologizing it was on such short notice. Mr Bo asked what he was going to do and he told him he was going away for a while, but that he'd be back. Mr Bo said nothing. He'd been reading the papers, too. The judge's decision had been in every newspaper in the Delta.

The next three days he worked with energy he never thought he possessed then on Thursday went to the bank and cashed his savings, almost five hundred dollars, the most money he'd ever seen in his life. At Pinkus Sklar's, a Jew who owned a surplus store with everything from suitcases to scissors, stuff he'd accumulated from attics, storage rooms, and garages, he bought a cheap Kodak camera that was in good working order and a valise to pack his belongings in and everything else he might need, the sum total not exceeding fifty dollars. He looked through the big sack Pinkus had put everything in, saw the camera and remembered one other item he'd need. He crossed the railroad tracks again and picked up a roll of film at the drug store. Mr Whiteside wished him well, asked if he'd ever heard back from his friend in Mexico. Not yet, but I aim to shortly, he said on his way out the door. He didn't forget the most important item he'd need. For a few dollars he got his Mississippi driver's license renewed at the Highway Patrol licensing bureau. This time he was going into the country legally.

He hitchhiked back to the Stevens' and packed the rest of the things he would need, then walked across the parking area and knocked on their door.

Looks like you're all ready for the road, Mr Bo said.

Bo'll drive you down to Drew, Miss Floy said. Wish you'd let us take you further.

No'me. I'll catch the bus in Drew. I would like to ask one favor of you, though.

Whatever we can do, Miss Floy said.

If you could be kind enough to keep my trunk and rest of my things. That'd be mighty helpful.

Consider it done, Mr Bo said.

Which way you going? Miss Floy said. She was still standing in the doorway. You might want to try west, she said, California. That's where everybody seems to be going these days, she said. He told her he didn't know but one direction and that was south. She stepped down onto the driveway and gave him a hug and wished him well. He threw his bag in the truck bed and got in, waved goodbye to her. As Mr Bo drove away he thought about why he'd said what he said. He knew there was a north and a west and an east. But south was all he'd ever heard, the only direction passed down through the generations of his family, as though there was none other. He'd have a family some day and his children and theirs would sit at his feet and ask him why he went south instead of west or east or north and he'd say that's where he needed to go. Then they'd ask the next question and he'd spin that long story one more time.

Mr Bo let him off on Main Street, wished him luck, told him to take care of himself and let them hear from him. Jo Shelby told him he would, that he even had their phone number written down.

He crossed the tracks and came to the Chinaman's grocery and decided there was one last trick he needed to play on fate. He went in and bought a Coke and Baby Ruth candy bar and kept walking until he came to the Greyhound bus depot on the highway.

Brownsville, Texas, one way, he said to the snaggle-tooth, stringy-haired woman on the other side of the glass window who glared at him as though he were some terrible menace sent to harass her and took damn near quarter of an hour figuring the itinerary and cost.

He sat outside on a bench, the day getting hotter, swelling like a balloon ready to burst. An hour later the bus from Memphis pulled in belching blue smoke from its rear. He gave his ticket to the driver and climbed aboard, took a front seat to himself. No other passengers were getting on and the driver quickly took his seat behind the large steering wheel, moved the gearshift through its motions and started off. Jo Shelby opened his valise and retrieved the letter from Senora Moncada and read it again. He'd never heard back from Carmen and could only hope she got the telegram and his letter and reclaimed the gun. He'd have never known if she was the one for him or not unless he'd come home. And he'd still never know if he didn't go back. The traveling a man has to do to find his heart, his place in life, to belong.

He thought of Athen and wished her well, glad they parted as they did, as friends, her testimony in court a confirmation before the world. Those were good memories, ones he would carry long and fondly through his life. He wished it could have been different, their lives together. They *were* two different people going in two different directions, different aims in life shaped by different histories. She got it damn right when she said they were trapped by the same thing, the only difference being she was getting out and he wasn't. He understood now why she wanted him to go with her to school, get a college degree, then her words that followed—make something of yourself, her voice bearing down hard on that last word, not the *make something*. Of the many voices trying to guide him, in that moment hers stood out, for none other spoke louder, or clearer. She'd helped him more than she knew and he thought of friends and how good it was to have them in life, to push up against to steady one's self. He still loved her more than a friend, hoped she still felt the same about him. She'd said they'd have to make their choices and see what happened. If she could see him now she might think different. He might not be completely out of the cage, but he was on his way.

A Memphis paper was lying on the wide dash and he asked the driver if he could read it and the driver nodded he could. The headlines shook his eyes: NEGRO BOY LYNCHED IN MISSISSIPPI. He read on, about a fourteen-year-old negro boy named Emmet Till from Chicago, how he was taken from his grandfather's home where he was visiting, in early morning hours, beaten and shot in the head, then his body wired with a gin fan and thrown into the Tallahatchie River. It had been there three days before anybody found it, which meant it happened early Sunday morning. He tried to keep reading but the words began to blur and he had to stop, glad he was sitting alone on the first row. And it happened, of all places, in Money, Mississippi.

He thought of Sissy and Jefferson and remembered he didn't say good-bye to them, then thought about their trapped world and its smallness and how close he came to making it bigger, might yet still. With her forward-looking vision he hoped Sissy, somehow, did see that coming. He put the paper down and rested his head against the seatback. It had been a long day and he welcomed the nap he felt tugging on him.

He dreamed and in his dream felt the strength of the horse beneath him, its compact stout flanks heaving against his legs, the smooth rhythm and roll of the ride, the furrowed ground sliding beneath him, the crisp night air against his face, the full moon rising, the hoof beats of another rider coming up fast behind him, then the night suddenly soundless and still and it was gone, his mind struggling in the darkness to bring it back. But all he saw when he opened his eyes was the sign on the small station that said Indianola and he moaned he was no farther along down the road.

The bus door swung open and the driver departed. Jo Shelby closed his eyes again, hoping to catch the dream and bring it back, ride it as long as he could when a voice said, Mind if I sit here? He opened his eyes, blinked several times, as if the batting of his lids might clear his vision, tell him which world he was in.

What? he said, his eyes still dazed.

I said do you mind if I sit here? she said.

The young lady was wearing sunglasses, a plain white T-shirt and blue jeans, hair in a ponytail and at first he didn't recognize her.

Athen?

She removed her sunglasses.

Athen. What the—

She reached over and placed a finger on his lips. Thought it might be prove interesting, us heading in the same direction for once. Besides, I couldn't let you go traipsing off to Mexico by yourself where some senorita might grab you. Now could I? She winked and slapped his knee playfully.

He swallowed hard.

The bus began pulling away. Visible through the adjacent window Mr Bo and Miss Floy standing beside their car, smiling and waving grandly.

He waved back to them. Well, if this doesn't beat all, he said, then leaned over and kissed her.

She put a hand over his and squeezed. He squeezed back and looked through the window, at the land, its neatly aligned rows passing swiftly by, at the stationary horizon that seemed to go nowhere, which was the Delta all right. And he was glad they were on a bus going somewhere, in the same direction. At least for the time being.

The End

ACKNOWLEDGEMENTS

Lester F. (Les) Sumners (6/2/1926-12/16/2005), my Boy Scout scoutmaster, mentor, personal attorney and confidante, three years before his death, happily accepted the task of walking me through all of the legal angles and nuances of deeds and wills. As well as courtroom demeanor, dynamics and the overarching umbrella of jurisprudence which hovered over the story. In the novel, he is Lester Darden, that last name belonging to his late partner at the time, Leslie Darden. I am indebted to Les, as he was affectionately called, not only for his unrelenting devotion to this book, but his emotional support and guidance through some difficult times. Thank you, Les, wherever you are.

SUE HERNER, my first agent, who, after publication of *Land Where My Fathers Died,* and before we agreed to separate, read and assisted with some of the revisions, particularly the more difficult scenes. I have lost touch with her, but if she is still alive, and sees this acknowledgement, I hope it touches and warms her heart.

PHYLLIS HARPER, (10/6/1933 — 2/12/2009) grand dame of north Mississippi writers, who read and helped edit the final revisions. Phyllis was also helpful with some of the genealogy and farming dynamics and terminology.

JOSEFINA RAYBURN, my Spanish teacher, who reviewed the final manuscript for corrections of Spanish, and read and edited the final revisions. She was also most helpful in assisting my navigation of the complex genealogical issues on both the American and Mexican sides of the families.

BRIAN HARGETT of the Lee County Library, reference librarian *extraordinaire,* continued, with great efficiency, to respond to every request and kept coming up with resource after resource on the Delta and farming, plus the dates when the moon was full, quarter or new.

Reagan and Minna Rothe and their Black Rose Writing staff for their continued support and willingness to take on the series project and their assistant in editing, cover design and promotion.

Jan Cobb, prominent artist and my map maker, for artistically producing another map better than the first one in the first edition in 2002. Thanks again, Jan, for providing maps for other books—*The Lost Page, The Lost Gospel* and the future publication of *The Lost Years.*

Sandi Perry Morris, for applying again her former English teaching editorial skills. But most importantly, along with her late parents Wiburn Perry (8/19/1914–4/21/2010) and Vera Cobb Perry (11/16/1916–10/31/2011) for teaching me more about farming, farm equipment, planting and harvest seasons than I had ever known and will ever know. I recall those evenings on their front porch when conversations of harrows, middle-busters, cotton picking, "popping Johns," etc., would continue on into the night. God bless you Wilburn and Vera and thank you for giving an abundance of wisdom far beyond the mechanics and seasons of farming that greatly helped this story, appropriately entitled *Inherit the Land.*

And thanks to my indispensable readers:

Peggy Webb, Francis Sheffield, John Corlew, W. O. "Bill" Rutledge III, Joe T. "Jo Jo" Wilkins III and these that have gone on before us: the late Dr. David White, Gerald Walton, Vera Perry, Beth and Henry Brevard, Bruce Smith, Betty Harrington, Martha Francis Allen,Francis Patterson, Bowen Burt, Cliff and Berylyn Davis, Larry Brown and Barry Hannah.

Lastly, and most fondly, to my late mother, Joan F. Morris, a strong and proud Ferguson, and my late father, William Edward Morris, good and unpretentious man and from whom I continue to drew inspiration for the character of Jo Shelby Ferguson.

ABOUT THE AUTHOR

Joe Edd Morris is the author of novels that include *Land Where My Fathers Died, The Prison, Torched: Summer of '64, The Lost Page and The Lost Gospel. Land Where My Fathers Died* and *The Prison,* were awarded Best Fiction of 2002 and 2020 respectively by the Mississippi Library Association. Joe Edd's non-fiction include *Ten Things I Wish Jesus Hadn't Said.* His short fiction has appeared in multiple literary journals with a nomination for the Pushcart Prize. Joe Edd is a psychologist and retired United Methodist minister. He and his wife, Sandi, live in Tupelo, MS where he has a psychology practice and enjoys, besides writing, traveling to places where the road ends, gardening and playing the piano.

OTHER TITLES BY JOE EDD MORRIS

FICTION

Land Where My Fathers Died

The Prison

Torched: Summer of '64

The Lost Page

The Lost Gospel

The Devil Walks at Midnight

NON-FICTION

Ten Things I Wish Jesus Hadn't Said

Old Testament Stories: What Do They Say Today?

New Testament Stories: What Do They Say Today?

Revival of the Gnostic Heresy: Fundamentalism

The Christian Right: Neither Christian Nor Right

Jury Selection in Mississippi: A Systematic Approach

NOTE FROM JOE EDD MORRIS

Word-of-mouth is crucial for any author to succeed. If you enjoyed *Inherit the Land*, please leave a review online—anywhere you are able. Even if it's just a sentence or two. It would make all the difference and would be very much appreciated.

Thanks!
Joe Edd Morris

We hope you enjoyed reading this title from:

BLACK❀ROSE
writing™

www.blackrosewriting.com

Subscribe to our mailing list – *The Rosevine* – and receive **FREE** books, daily deals, and stay current with news about upcoming releases and our hottest authors.
Scan the QR code below to sign up.

Already a subscriber? Please accept a sincere thank you for being a fan of Black Rose Writing authors.

View other Black Rose Writing titles at
www.blackrosewriting.com/books and use promo code
PRINT to receive a **20% discount** when purchasing.

www.ingramcontent.com/pod-product-compliance
Lightning Source LLC
Chambersburg PA
CBHW051226210726
48290CB00003B/828